UNEXPECTED GUEST

He went into the kitchen, expecting to find Veline there, but she, too, seemed to have disappeared. Feeling let down, he was turning to leave when he heard a woman's scream from upstairs. He froze in his tracks. The sound had not been one of fright; rather, it was the sound of pure ecstasy. He stood there a moment longer before he turned swiftly toward the stairs.

When he reached the bedroom door, he saw them, their nude bodies gleaming with perspiration, entangled together in an unnatural position.

She was getting what she wanted now, he thought. He felt strangely elated.

He paused a moment, breathing deeply. He would be unable to keep his date with Lynne. She had been so eager in her passion and had promised so much. Too bad, he thought.

He opened the bedroom door and unhurriedly walked inside . . .

Episode in a Town

Jay Carr

WILDSIDE PRESS

one

HARRY MERCER saw Beach City for the first time on a Friday afternoon while driving south from Los Angeles. He crested a hill, swung slightly to the right, and there it was, nestled between a blue crescent bay and a cluster of craggy peaks that seemed to push themselves into the center of the town itself. He pulled his car over to the side of the road and stopped and smoked a cigarette and had his look.

He had seen the Beach City *Times* advertisement in *Editor & Publisher* while visiting his sister and her family near Chicago. The next thing he knew, he had committed himself to the job. Actually, he had wanted to return to Europe, but the post he had had there had blown up and he needed money. Besides, he didn't know anybody in Beach City—and the one thing he coveted more than anything else was privacy and solitude. And so here he was.

He followed the main highway into the middle of the downtown district, noting the many different kinds of trees lining the streets, oak and pine and cabbage palm and eucalyptus and royal palm. He was pleased with the trees; they gave him a comfortable, almost a welcome, feeling.

He stopped and asked directions to the *Times* building, then made a left turn, crossed the railroad tracks that paralleled the highway and the beach, and found what he was looking for. He was slightly surprised at the size of the concrete, two-storied building; he had not expected it to be that large.

He parked in the almost empty lot next to the building, straightened his tie, ran a hand through his tight curly hair, and then got out of the car and walked inside. The little blond teen-ager behind the reception desk put aside her movie magazine and gave him a brief, tired smile.

"I'd like to see Mr. Hennings," he said.

"I'm sorry, sir. The editorial offices are closed now."

He looked at the clock on the wall: four-twenty.

"Has Mr. Hennings gone home?"

"I'm sorry, sir," she said. "I'm not supposed to ring Mr. Hennings after four o'clock."

"May I use your phone? I'll call him. I've driven all the way from Los Angeles to see him. He's expecting me."

She sighed, asked him to sit down, and then picked up the phone and dialed. She spoke a few words in a low voice.

"Mr. Hennings will see you now," she said, a surprised look on her face. "Just go up those stairs."

He followed the steps up to the second floor and saw that this part of the building was taken up by the editorial offices, and again he was surprised by the bigness of it all, considering the size of Beach City.

Through an open door at the left he saw a bank of linotype machines, but in the room where he was, desks lined the left wall with the city editor's horseshoe desk in the middle, more desks with typewriters on them running up the middle of the room and, at the far end, a glassed-in room with two or three teletype machines in it and several more desks. At the far right, two sections were partitioned off from each other by ceiling-high wooden screens and from the rest of the room by waist-high wooden railings; there was a glassed-in cubicle at the right-front, immediately in front of him. Three men were visible to him, one with his back to him in the glassed-in room at the far end, another in the nearest partition to the right, had his feet up on a desk, his face turned quizzically towards Harry, while the third man stood before the glassed-in cubicle, looking expectantly at Harry.

He was a little man, wearing a dark-blue suit and a starched white shirt. He was about fifty and, apparently, meticulous about his dress; his black shoes had a high polish, almost matching the shine on his bald head, and his wine-red tie was centered exactly in the middle of his collar; he looked uncomfortable but happy, and Harry guessed that was the most important thing, after all.

"Mr. Mercer?" the man said, extending his hand.

"Yes," Harry replied, taking the hand, grasping it briefly.

"I'm Mr. Hennings. Come in."

Harry followed him into the small office. Hennings closed the door. The office was like the man himself, meticulously neat. It made Harry think immediately of an old saying his father used to quote to him: "A place for everything and everything in its place."

There was no clutter on the desk. Two spikes on brass standards both skewered several pieces of copy paper; a two-tiered wooden stand, the top marked IN and the bottom marked OUT, both empty; about a dozen thick yellow copy pencils, all freshly sharpened; an expensive-looking cigarette lighter which looked massive enough to actually work; a huge round ceramic ashtray, clean; and a gold-framed photograph of a tired-looking woman and two equally tired-looking little girls.

"I'm sorry to have caught you so late in the day," Harry said after they had both seated themselves. "I don't know why, but I assumed the *Times* was a morning paper."

"That's quite all right," said Hennings. "No. We found a long time ago that we couldn't compete with the bigger morning papers from Los Angeles, so we switched to the afternoon. Most people here take one of the Los Angeles papers in the morning, but almost everyone subscribes to the *Times* in the afternoon. He smiled a crisp little smile. "You're somewhat early, Mr. Mercer. We weren't expecting you until next week."

"I got into Los Angeles yesterday," Harry said. "I don't like Los Angeles. I didn't want to spend any more time there than was necessary."

"That's understandable. Then you've been out here before? To California, I mean?"

"Oh, yes."

"Have you ever been in Beach City before, Mr. Mercer?"

"No, not to my knowledge."

"Well," Hennings said and smiled that crisp little smile again, "I'm sure you would have remembered it if you had been here. We take considerable pride in our small city."

"I can see why, Mr. Hennings. It's a very beautiful place."

"Yes, that's true, but we have more than just beauty here, Mr. Mercer. We have a way of life."

Harry said nothing to that; he did not know what he could say.

Hennings opened his top desk drawer, took out an envelope, pulled out the letter, glanced at it a moment, and then at Harry.

"Just refreshing myself a bit on your history," he said. "You've been around quite a bit, Mr. Mercer."

"Yes. I like to travel."

"Well, we like to think our employees here at the *Times* will be permanent, or at least semi-permanent. I realize if an offer for a better position came along you couldn't turn it down, and I wouldn't expect you to, but I wouldn't want you to work here six months and then skip out for no good reason."

"I thought the job was settled."

"It is."

"You're not talking that way, Mr. Hennings. You're talking as if I'm here for an interview. Your letter in answer to my application stated that I met the qualifications, that I had the job, and I came out here on that assumption."

"Your assumption is correct, Mr. Mercer. The job is yours. However, I thought I'd better state my position a little more clearly."

"I can understand that."

"We seem to be going off on the wrong foot."

"Yes, we do."

"You're a hard-headed young man, aren't you, Mr. Mercer?" His quick smile had lost some of its crispness. "I don't mean to offend you in any way."

"You're not offending me."

"Good. I want us to understand each other, and have that understanding right from the beginning. I'm editor, publisher and owner of this paper, Mr. Mercer, and I run it quietly, the way I see fit to run it. I like Beach City, I like the people who live here, and I make my home here and hope that my children will make their home here. It's a quiet town, nothing much happens here, and that's why I run a quiet newspaper. I feel I owe that much to the subscribers and the way I feel, I usually act. There's no hanky-panky about it. I was young once, like you, and I liked to wander around, like you, and I'm hard-headed, again like you, and I'm telling you this because you'll probably hear it from the first bastard you meet, anyway, so it might as well come from me. Do you drink?"

"I usually get drunk at least once every two weeks."

Hennings laughed, a surprising sound.

"As long as you don't drink on the job, that's all I ask. I think you know the pay, I mentioned it in the letter—one-twenty a week and we have a very good hospitalization plan. If you have to work overtime, which happens occasionally, that's your problem, and not mine. Your work will be general reporting and you'll be under Henry Grayson, our city editor. I said before, Beach City is a quiet place and we do everything we can here at the

Times to keep it that way. One or two or three murders a year, that's about all. The usual traffic problems, and a few knifings down in Mexican-town, and maybe a strike at the aircraft plant, in which case we very carefully try to tell our subscribers that management is in the right, though we don't preach sermons and never have. In case of rape, which very rarely happens, we never mention the name of the injured woman. We support the Republican Party in both national and local elections and are proud to do so."

"I think I understand."

"I hope you do, Mr. Mercer. It's very important that you do."

"When do I start?"

"You can start Monday if you like, or you can wait until a week from Monday, the original date agreed upon. Take your pick."

"I'd just as soon start this Monday."

"Do you have a place to live?"

"No. I came straight here."

"There's a good hotel two blocks up Arguello—the Seaside. It's inexpensive and they have a fair restaurant and a bar that sometimes gets the tourist trade this time of the year. I'm sure that will appeal to you. We get a lot of tourist trade during the spring and the summer and it's always seemed to me that the bulk of it is nice young ladies with nothing to do but sit on the beach during the day and sit on a bar stool during the night. You look like a healthy young man with a healthy appetite."

"I think I'm going to like working for you, Mr. Hennings."

"I'm sure you will. I'm a helluva nice guy to work for."

They both laughed.

Hennings said, "I'd ask you to dinner at my house tonight, but we're going out and I don't believe in mixing socially with my employees. You can take that for what it's worth. I have two other very hard and fast rules,

Mr. Mercer, and they are, not necessarily in order of importance, that you never swear in front of the women reporters and that you always call me *Mister* Hennings. I insist upon both of them, and I'm sure you won't mind."

"Of course not."

"Fine." Hennings rose. "I'll see you Monday morning, then."

Harry started to leave.

"One question, Mr. Mercer," Hennings said. "If it's none of my business, tell me so."

"Yes?"

"You're a man with a good education and a fine background and your past employers have all given you excellent references. What do you want in a place like Beach City?"

"What makes you think I want anything?"

"We all want something."

"Perhaps."

"I was very intrigued by your application and, frankly, quite anxious to meet you. I feel you could be doing bigger and better things."

"Possibly, Mr. Hennings. But that's true of just about everyone. Bigger and better things."

Hennings laughed. "I guess it is."

Thomas Joseph Howard Hennings was, to all intents and purposes, a successful man. He had tracked down success in the same way that a good hunter tracks down his intended victim, combining a certain amount of cold-bloodedness with an equal amount of empathy. The man was fifty-two years old, had arrived in Beach City in 1938 with enough money to buy a struggling weekly newspaper and enough gall and drive to turn it into a successful small-town daily, and had never been farther away than Los Angeles—some seventy-two miles—in all the years since. He had married Margaret Ann Wallace, the oldest daughter of one of Beach City's oldest and most respected families, in 1942, and they now had two daughters of their own, Anne Elizabeth, age twelve, and Mary Jean, age nine. He was a member of the country club and the beach club and the Lions and the chamber of commerce and the board of education, and he was very adamant in his love for Beach City. He had done only one thing in his life that he was really ashamed of, and not even his wife knew anything about that, and no one ever would know anything about it, God willing. In 1936, in a small town in western Massachusetts, Sydney Howard von Hock had had his name legally changed to Thomas Joseph Howard Hennings; he had kept the Howard out of some respect for his dead mother. Even to this day, he could remember the presiding judge looking down at him, frowning, looking away, frowning again, and then granting the name change; the judge's name had· been Goldstein.

Now, as he turned into the driveway and stopped his car and got out, he was still thinking about his talk with Harry Mercer. The man intrigued him in a way that he had not been intrigued in a long time. He could not explain it. There was nothing really outstanding about Mercer; he was just a young man who had been a lot of places and done a lot of things, and now he was here in Beach City and his attitude seemed to state that he didn't give a damn one way or the other whether he stayed or not, and Thomas Joseph Howard Hennings could not understand this attitude.

His wife, Margaret, was just putting down the phone as he entered the living room, and Mary Jean was curled up on the couch, her eyes reddened and swollen. Margaret turned and looked at him and tried to smile and he thought how tired she looked and wondered about that; she was only thirty-seven, and she should not look so tired all the time. He kissed her on the cheek and kissed his daughter on the forehead and then sat down and sighed a big sigh.

"You look tired, Thomas," his wife said.

He almost laughed; he had been about to say that to her.

"I am tired," he said. "It was a long day."

"That was Grace on the phone. She's going to be fifteen minutes late."

"She's always late, Margaret."

"But she always calls."

"That doesn't excuse her lateness." He turned, looking at his daughter, who had remained curled up on the couch. "And what's the matter with little Miss Mary Jean tonight?"

"She's been crying again," Mrs. Hennings said.

"I can see that."

"She's upset."

"Well, she must be upset or she wouldn't have cried. What is it, Mary Jean?"

Mary Jean did not answer. She was a small child, frail, seemingly all knees and elbows, and her face was dominated by an overly large nose and she had a habit of continually rubbing the back of her hand across her nose, as if trying to push it back into her face.

"Mary Jean, your father asked you something," Mrs. Hennings said.

"I—I heard him," the girl stammered.

"Then answer him."

"I don't wanna answer him."

"Don't slur your words, Mary Jean. You're old—"

"Margaret," he said, "don't make a scene. Mary Jean, go to your room."

Mary Jean got up without a word and pattered out of the room and, presently, he heard her door slamming.

"She cries too much," he said.

"I've said that many times."

"Perhaps we should do something about it."

"Like what?"

"I don't know like what. Have you told Dr. Goodman about her crying all the time?"

"He says all nine-year-old girls cry all the time."

"Does he know what he's saying?"

"How would I know?"

"Well, did you cry a lot then?"

"I can't remember that far back, Thomas." She smiled. "You know my life began when I met you."

He laughed. "I'd like a drink."

She said, "I made manhattans."

"That's all right."

"I could make martinis."

"No, Margaret, a manhattan will be fine."

"The last time I made them, you didn't like them."

"That was the last time. I'll have one now."

She left and then came back and handed him his drink and sat down with her own.

"Where's Anne?"

"I told her she could stay all night with the Hendersons."

He sipped his drink. It was not very good and he did not like manhattans, anyway; but Grace was coming by, and he knew his wife would have made them for Grace, so he kept silent about it.

"The new man came today."

"Oh? What's his name?"

"Harry Mercer."

"Is he?—"

"No, Margaret, he isn't married."

"What does he look like?"

"He looks like all the other young men you've ever seen, Margaret. All young men look alike. He's thirty-two or thirty-three, I forget which, and sort of tallish, and he squints a little and frowns too much, and he's quite bull-headed, and he was in the war and has worked on different papers in this country and Europe and I'm sure Grace wouldn't like him."

"I didn't say anything about Grace."

"I know you didn't say anything about Grace. I said something about Grace. I said Grace wouldn't like him, and I'm sure she wouldn't. He appears to be a young man with a mind of his own, and any man like that wouldn't appeal to Grace."

She smiled. "Grace is my sister, Thomas."

"I know she's your sister, Margaret, your little sister. She's what now? Twenty-five? And wilting on the vine or whatever proper trite phrase applies to unmarried young women of twenty-five. And you're worried that she'll still be wilting on that same vine ten years from now and you don't want her to wilt on that vine, so every time we meet or hear of a new eligible young man in town you immediately begin thinking of Grace. Don't, Margaret. Not this time. He's working for me and you know I don't like mixing with people who work for me and I don't know how else they could possibly meet."

"Thomas," she said, laughing, "you're impossible."

"Isn't that why you married me?"

"You know why I married you."

"If I weren't so old and those stairs weren't so steep, you'd find out why you married me. I'd refresh your memory."

"My memories are still fresh enough."

"I hope so, Margaret, I hope so."

"Thomas, I only wish Grace could find someone half as good as you, and then I wouldn't have to worry about her."

"Then you admit it?"

"Yes, I admit it. I do worry."

"Let her lead her own life, Margaret. She appears to be happy enough."

"How can she be happy? It's not a natural life, the life she leads. A woman is supposed to be with a man, and she has no man, and so she can't be happy."

"Your logic escapes me. Anyway, how do we know she

doesn't have a man? She could be shacking up with someone on the side and we wouldn't know a thing about it."

"I would, too. And besides, Grace wouldn't go to bed with a man unless she was married to him."

"You did."

"What I did and what she does are two different things."

"I'm glad of that."

He finished his drink and got up and said, "I'd better have a talk with Mary Jean. I guess I haven't time for a shower, have I?"

"You take too many showers, Thomas. You're the cleanest, absolutely the cleanest, man I've ever known."

"Is that so?" he said, and left the room.

His daughter was lying on her stomach on her bed in her pink-and-white bedroom that was hers alone, her face half-buried in a pillow. She was looking at the door with one open eye when her father came in, and she immediately turned her head the other way and kicked her heels up in the air.

"All right, Mary Jean," he said, sitting down on the edge of the bed.

She rolled over on her back and looked up at him with those big round eyes that reminded him so much of his own mother, and smiled suddenly.

"Did I make a scene, Daddy?"

"Yes, Mary Jean, you made a scene. But how many times have I asked you not to call me Daddy?"

"I dunno. A million, I guess."

"How many is a million?"

"Five zeroes. No, *six* zeroes."

"That's right, and that's quite a few times, isn't it? And yet you still call me that. You're old enough now, Mary Jean, to call me Father and I want you to call me Father. Can you understand that?"

"Yes, I can understand that—Father."

"That's better. Now, what was the crying about this time?"

"I don't wanna talk about it."

"Why not?"

"I dunno."

"You must know, Mary Jean. You were crying, so you must know why."

"Why must I?"

"You just must, that's all."

"You really wanna know, Da—Father?"

"Yes, I really want to know, Mary Jean."

"I'm going in B-Five this year."

"I know that."

She was silent.

"Is that why you were crying? You don't want to go into B-Five?"

"I dunno."

"Please, Mary Jean." He put a hand out, stroking her forehead. "Don't be like this with me. I've worked hard all day and I'm tired."

"I'm sorry you're tired, Father."

"Tell me."

"Aunt Grace teaches B-five."

"I see," he said.

"I don't wanna be in Aunt Grace's class. It wouldn't be fair to the other kids."

"Children," he said absently, getting to his feet.

"Is that so bad, Daddy?"

He looked down at her and shook his head. "No. No, that isn't so bad, Mary Jean."

"I sorta think it is, Daddy. I sorta think it is very much bad. I love Aunt Grace, but gosh, you know, I remember Jimmie Brown was in B-Four and his mother was teaching him and all the kids made fun of him and I don't wanna be made fun of, like Jimmie Brown was."

"I understand, Mary Jean," he said.

"You always do, Daddy. I can't talk to Mummy the way I talk to you, Daddy. Why?"

"Well, maybe it's because your mother is here all day and I'm not. Your mother loves you very much, Mary Jean." He bent down, kissing her on the forehead. "Mrs. Simms will give you your dinner tonight. We're going out."

"Daddy, I love you."

"I love you, too, Mary Jean. Very much."

Hennings had never particularly liked Tiscareno's Sea Grill, but Margaret and Grace both liked it and so they made a practice of dining there about once every two weeks. Raul Tiscareno was a fat little Mexican who, somehow or other, always managed to smell of incense, and this bothered Hennings; he didn't mind the smell of garlic or fish or onions, and he would have expected that; but for the past fifteen years once every two weeks, he and Margaret and Grace—sometimes with a date for Grace, sometimes not—would dine at Tiscareno's Sea Grill on the end of the pier and he would have to smell Raul Tiscareno and his incense. He wondered if anyone else had ever noticed that smell; he doubted it; it would be something that only he would notice; he had a faculty for noticing such things. He would much rather dine at either the country club or the beach club —and he and Margaret did quite often—but ever since Felipe Nevarez had had his application for membership turned down at both clubs, Grace had refused to enter either one.

The Nevarez family was the oldest family in Beach City; it could be traced back to the Spanish Land Grant days and, though he had never personally verified this, there was a rumor that the first Nevarez had once owned all the land upon which Beach City now stood. Nevertheless, the clubs had had to take a stand against Mexicans in general; if Felipe Nevarez had been admitted, then someone like Raul Tiscareno could eventually get in, and then all the Sanchezes and the Garcias and the Martinezes and the Esquedas and all the rest. And, naturally, they couldn't allow that—"they" being the present members of the country club and the beach club.

He looked at his sister-in-law now and, as always, felt somewhat humble in the face of her beauty. She was, without a doubt, just about the most strikingly beautiful woman he had ever known personally, and he had watched that beauty form and mature over the years. She was twelve years younger than his wife, and the relationship between Margaret and Grace was a peculiar one, more like that between a mother and daughter than between two sisters. He could understand this, but at times it still was a source of irritation with him.

Mrs. Wallace had died when Grace was but two years old; Mr. Wallace had been fifty-six when Grace was born, and had taken little or no interest in either one of his daughters. As a result, the relationship had developed into the mother-daughter thing and now Hennings had to put up with it and he tried to make the best of it, not always succeeding. He had often wondered about Grace's sex life, if she had any at all. He found it hard to believe that a woman with her beauty could remain aloof from the physical side of life. He had never coveted her; he was completely satisfied with Margaret and always had been, and there never had been room for another woman in his life. Margaret was all he wanted, but he knew the depths of her passions and imagined that the same depths ran in Grace. There had been a series of young men over the years, ranging from Jack Perkins, of the Perkins banking family, to Ramon Nevarez, son of Felipe, to Jim Harris, the football star, and to many others. The dating with Ramon had caused quite a bit of gossip and he had known, at the time, that it had also caused Margaret an immense amount of concern; but that was in the past now, and Grace, at present, did not seem greatly interested in anyone in particular.

Now he looked at his watch and noted that it was a

little after ten o'clock. Margaret saw him looking at his watch, smiled, and nodded her head, and he knew she understood. He had a rule about always being in bed by midnight and he had missed that goal only once during their married life. That had been when Mary Jean was born; she had come into the world at 2:15 A.M., and he had stayed at the hospital until that time.

There seemed to be a lull in the conversation between Margaret and Grace, so he said: "Mary Jean is quite upset about the prospect of having you for a teacher this fall, Grace."

"You didn't tell me that, Thomas," Mrs. Hennings said.

"Didn't I? I thought I did."

"I can understand her point," said Grace.

"Can you?" asked Mrs. Hennings.

"Of course," Grace said. "I think it's perfectly understandable. Mary Jean is a highly sensitive child. She's nine years old and the nine-year-old period is an extremely difficult one."

"I thought they were all difficult," he said.

Grace laughed. "Well, I guess they are."

"They are from birth to twelve," said Mrs. Hennings. "I can speak from experience on that."

"At any rate," said Grace, "I think I know how Mary Jean feels and I sympathize with her. I wasn't teaching when Anne went through fifth grade, so—"

"It wouldn't have bothered Anne, anyway," he said.

"Nothing bothers Anne," Mrs. Hennings said.

"—so Mary Jean now has to face a new difficulty. I have given the problem some thought, trying to work out something, but I'm sorry to say I can't come up with any solution."

"I have one," Mrs. Hennings said. "We could send Mary Jean to a private school, to Miss Johnson's."

"Oh, nonsense," said Grace.

"I agree with Grace," said Hennings. "I don't believe in private schools, and you know that, Margaret."

"Grace and I both went to Miss Johnson's," Mrs. Hennings said. "It didn't do us any harm, did it?"

"Well, I can't vouch for that," Hennings said. "I don't think there is any solution. She'll just have to face the problem and make the best of it. I'm sure she will."

"I'm sure she will, too," Grace said.

"She's such a cry-baby, though," Mrs. Hennings said.

The coffee and brandy came, interrupting them momentarily.

He said, "Isn't that your friend Cynthia Ross over there, Grace?"

Both women turned and looked, and Grace nodded. "Yes," she said.

"I don't see John anywhere," Mrs. Hennings said.

"Who's that with her?" Hennings asked.

"Carl Morris," Grace said.

"Who's he?" Mrs. Hennings asked.

"A friend of the family," Grace said.

"He's not Beach City," Mrs. Hennings said.

"No. They met him in Los Angeles, I think."

"I think it's funny that John's not with them."

"Don't gossip, Margaret," Grace said.

"I wasn't gossiping. I just said I thought it was funny. I can say that and not be gossiping, can't I? I think it is funny, going out to dinner with a man and not having your husband along. I wouldn't do it, believe me."

"There are a lot of things you wouldn't do, Margaret," Hennings said, "that are done by millions of people every day in the week."

"He looks German," Mrs. Hennings said. "Is Morris a German name, Thomas? Or perhaps Jewish?"

"I wouldn't know."

"Is it, Grace?"

"How would I know? What difference does it make, anyway?"

"Well, none, I guess. I don't know."

"It's getting late, Margaret," Hennings said.

"I know," she said.

"There's a man over there at the bar looking at you as if he knows you, Thomas," Grace said.

He turned and saw Harry Mercer standing alone by the bar. Mercer nodded and Hennings nodded back, then raised a hand, inviting Mercer over. Hennings rose and shook hands and then said: "Mr. Mercer, this is my wife, Mrs. Hennings, and her sister, Miss Wallace."

"How do you do?" Harry said.

The two women nodded.

There was a tight little smile on Harry Mercer's mouth. "I don't want to interfere, Mr. Hennings. I remember about your rule."

"Thomas is famous for his little rules," Grace said. She was smiling.

"I imagined he would be," Harry said.

Hennings laughed, and said, "Sit down, Mr. Mercer. We're just finishing our coffee and brandy. I'll bend the rule a little this time."

"That's very kind of you," Harry said, with the sarcasm there for all to hear.

"Mr. Mercer is a new reporter on the paper," Hennings said. "He just got here today."

"Oh?" said Grace. "Where are you from, Mr. Mercer?"

"Here," he said.

"But I thought Thomas said you just got here today."

"I did. But I'm here now, and so I'm from here now. Beach City is my home."

Hennings wondered if the man had been drinking too much. He didn't look as if he had been, but then you couldn't always tell by the way someone looked. He didn't like Mercer's tone, not a bit. It was one thing to be bull-headed or hard-headed or whatever you wanted to call it, and quite another thing to be just plain rude.

"What have you been doing with yourself tonight, Mr. Mercer?" he asked.

"Nothing much. I checked in at that hotel you recommended, had dinner there and a couple of drinks in that dark little hole they call a bar and didn't see anything interesting so I went to another bar and then another, and now I'm here. It's been a goddamned boring— oh, excuse me, Mr. Hennings; I almost forgot about that other rule, but then they're not reporters, are they?— a very boring evening."

Grace laughed. Mrs. Hennings put her hand up to her mouth, hiding the smile there.

"I think maybe you've had too many drinks," Hennings said.

"Maybe I have, at that. I told you I get drunk at least once every two weeks, and I think it's been about that long since the last time."

"Mr. Mercer," Mrs. Hennings said, "maybe you could help me. I asked both my husband and my sister if Morris was a Jewish name, and neither of them knew."

"Margaret!" Grace snapped.

"Oh, that's all right," Harry said. "I don't mind. I don't happen to be Jewish and I can't see what difference it would make if I were. As a matter of fact, though, Mrs. Hennings, I think I can help you out a little on the subject. Actually, the name Morris has been changed from its original meaning. You see, back in the days of good King Arthur and his Merry Men—or was that Robin Hood?—at any rate, back in those days, there was a very pretty young damsel named . . . let me see, named Anne More, yes, that was it, and old King Arthur took a liking to her and the obvious thing happened that always happened between good old King Arthur and any pretty young damsel he happened to like and he used to stand up on his stone balcony—I think it was stone, though it might have been something else—and yell More Ass, More Ass, but Queen Whatever-Her-Name-Was thought that was a bad influence on all the little princes and princesses they had running around the castle—and

I'm sure we'd all agree with her on that—and insisted that he not yell that so he changed it to More-As and then to More-Is and then finally to Morris."

The two women laughed, Mrs. Hennings a little nervously.

Hennings said, "It's really late, Margaret. I think we'd better be going."

Grace said, "I'm very happy to have met you, Mr. Mercer. Perhaps we'll meet again."

"I don't doubt that one bit," he said. "Not one bit."

two

GRACE WALLACE heard the sounds of the party through the bathroom door. She took another look at herself in the mirror, poked fingers at her hair, and wondered how soon she could safely leave if she expelled the gas now, if they would hear her in the other part of the house. She tried to remember ever hearing anyone else do that, and couldn't. But she did remember the time Cynthia had done it before the whole class in the tenth grade. Poor Cynthia. It had been absolutely the worst thing that had ever happened to her. She felt so sorry for poor Cynthia, remembering the incident; she would never be able to live down a thing like that. How could she?

The sounds in the other part of the house grew in intensity. She stood there, leaning against the wash basin, and stared at the pretty pink walls and listened to the sounds, and tried to expel the gas at the same time, and failed. She shook her head and said, "Damn." She should have known better than to have tried some of that cheese dip with the onions in it; onions always gave her gas. She had been in the bathroom for almost five minutes now.

Harry certainly would be missing her by now, even with that bitchy Bess Higgins playing up to him the way she was. She could picture him, the way his face would turn toward the hall door leading to the bathroom. He would frown, mutter something under his breath, and frown some more. She had told him about that frowning habit; it wasn't good for someone his age because he would have lines on his forehead, permanent ones, before he was even thirty-five. She laughed, suddenly. She wasn't sure he wasn't already thirty-five. Actually, when you came right down to it, she wasn't sure of much about him, other than that she was determined to marry him; and she did not want any man she was going to marry to have lines on his forehead. She had met him just a week ago yesterday, Friday, when Thomas had introduced them at Tiscareno's.

Someone tried to open the bathroom door. She yelled, "Occupied," and whoever it was went away. She had an idea who it was, too—Carl Morris. It would be like him to try something like that. He wasn't above anything like that. If the door had not been locked, he would have walked in, looked surprised, and excused himself. But he would have had his look, and she knew that was what he wanted. She did not like Carl Morris, never had liked him, and never would. He gave her a queasy kind of feeling, a feeling she could not really explain, not even to herself. Oh, he was handsome enough, taller even than Harry, and from the way he spent money, he certainly must have some, though no one knew exactly what he did. Carl Morris was a friend of Cynthia's, someone she had met in Los Angeles—Hollywood, to be more exact—and he was also a friend of Frank Manning, the movie star, and he spent a lot of time with Frank Manning or so he said. Other than that, no one seemed to know much about him. He was always invited to all the parties; he gave them a certain distinction, the way he could talk about movie stars. There was something about his eyes, the way he would look at a girl—not only her, but any girl. She had a secret suspicion about Carl Morris, one she had never told anyone, but she had an idea that Carl Morris was the kind of man who kept those dirty little books, and looked at them all the time.

She smiled then. That was her picture of Carl Morris. She would have to tell Cynthia about that. But no. She suddenly thought of the rumors about Cynthia and Carl Morris; she did not believe the rumors, but she had seen Cynthia and Carl together, alone, at Tiscareno's. No. On second thought, she hadn't better tell Cynthia.

She sat down on the toilet seat, crossed her legs, and looked at her watch. She would give herself another five minutes. If she hadn't done it by then, she would just have to take her chances. There was another bathroom, so she wouldn't be holding anyone up. But she could not leave Harry sitting out there, talking to that bitchy Bess Higgins. She knew what kind of a person Bess Higgins was, and she didn't want Harry talking to her for too long. The talk could lead to something else, and she wanted that something else for herself.

But, of course, at the proper time.

Harry emptied his drink and clicked his tongue against the roof of his mouth, and stared back at Bess Higgins. He was bored by the party, by these people, though not by Bess Higgins in particular, but by the rest of them. If he had known what it was going to be, he would never have come with Grace. True, they were her friends, and she was okay, but he never had enjoyed spending his evenings with car salesmen and insurance men and accountants and young bankers on their way up and all their wives and would-be wives. They didn't know a damn thing that they were trying to talk about, whether it was politics or sex or religion or the latest book club selection or the new movies or babies—although, admittedly, he knew nothing about babies—and what griped him was that they were all so positive in their thinking. He did not like positive people; he was positive himself, but, of course, he made an exception for himself and discounted the rest of them.

He turned slightly to look at the hall door again, frowning, wondering what Grace was doing in there for so long. Maybe—no, he did not like that thought. He had determined that this was to be the night and nothing she would be able to say would change that; nothing, that is, except an attack of what he sometimes called lunar trouble. He frowned again, and looked back at Bess Higgins who was still staring at him.

"She's been gone a long time," Bess said. "Maybe she fell in."

"Maybe she did."

"Want me to check?"

"Of course not."

"Your drink is empty."

"It can stay empty. I've had enough."

"How can you tell when you've had enough?"

"I get mean and nasty."

"I don't think you could ever be—mean and nasty, I mean."

"I know what you mean."

She threw back her head and laughed. She did everything with a large amount of gusto. She was a big woman, tall and tending slightly towards heaviness, with huge breasts and an over-abundance of reddish hair that she made no effort to control.

"What's so funny?"

"You are, Harry. But you're a darling, too, an absolute darling."

"So I'm a darling and I'm also funny?"

"So I can read your mind."

"Can you?"

"Oh, yes."

The other guests were milling around them, paying not

the slightest bit of attention to them. There were, perhaps, twenty people in attendance. Cynthia Ross, sur-
rounded by a group near the south wall, stood beneath the
four abstract watercolors, chattering, chattering, chattering. Someone—he looked up to see John Ross, Cynthia's
husband—took the empty glass out of his hand.

"You disappoint me, Harry," Bess said. "I thought all
newspapermen were hard drinkers."

"An illusion," he said, "planted by television and the
movies."

She smiled, and said, "You're not going to get it from
li'l ol' Miss Grace Wallace this night."

He didn't answer. He was watching John Ross wend his
way through the people toward the bar in the corner.

"What does John Ross do?"

"He has the Lincoln-Mercury agency," she said.

"I'll bet he watches Ed Sullivan every Sunday night."

"I'll bet he does, too."

"I didn't mean anything by that. He's a nice guy."

"Who? Sullivan or John?"

"John."

"The world is full of nice guys."

"And nice women."

"I'm a nice woman, Harry."

"That's not what I hear."

"Oh, you hear a lot of things. I've been married and
divorced twice, so you hear a lot of things. Besides, it depends what you mean by nice. It's an over-used word."

"Why have you been divorced twice?"

"If I could answer that," she said, "I might not have
gotten the first divorce."

"Then you got it?"

"He certainly didn't, the little crumb."

"The first one?"

"Yes, the first one."

"Sounds like—"

"Doesn't sound like anything, Harry, dear. We're getting off the track."

"What track?"

"The track about you and lil'l ol' Miss Gracie."

"I didn't know we were on that track."

"Well, we were. I said—"

"I know what you said."

"—I said you're not going to get it from her this night. As a matter of fact, Harry dear, I don't think you'll get it from her any night, not unless you do the obvious."

"And what's that?"

"The bells—the wedding bells."

He wanted to say something to that but could not think of anything to say so he kept his mouth shut. John Ross was coming back with a drink, and he knew the drink would be for him, and he knew he would drink it. He never got mean and nasty; it was something he had just said, and he wondered why he had said it. He saw Grace returning from the bathroom and there was a sort of satisfied look on her face and his hopes rose. She was awfully damn beautiful, almost too beautiful to be real.

"I'll be home later," Bess said, very quickly.

John and Grace got there at the same time. He noted that John was slightly drunk, and he knew why. With a wife like Cynthia, the only thing for a man to do was to get drunk.

"The drinks are to drink," John said, handing Harry the full glass.

"I'm sorry I was so long—darling," said Grace, staring hard at Bess Higgins.

"I was wondering," Harry said.

"Never wonder about a woman, Harry," said John.

"When you quit wondering about women," said Bess "you might as well roll over and be dead."

"I've heard that about you," said Grace.

"Heard what?"

"That you roll over a lot."

Bess laughed. "My, my."

Harry said, "It's awfully damned hot in here."

"The air conditioning broke down," said John.

"How long is this thing going to last?" asked Harry.

"As long as there's anyone around to listen to her," said John, pointing at his wife. "You listen, she talks."

"I don't think that's quite fair, John," said Grace.

"You wouldn't," said Bess.

"I think I'll look at the garden," said John. "We don't have a garden, but I think I'll look at it, all the same. Care to join me, Bess?"

"I don't care to, but I guess I have to."

They moved away together. Harry watched her walk away. She had a nice walk. The invitation had been there before, and he stored that away for future reference.

He told Grace, "I don't think you were very nice to her."

"That's a funny thing for you to say. You're not nice to many people."

"I don't like many people."

"Besides, I didn't intend being nice to her."

"Why not?"

"She's a bitch, Harry."

"I don't think so."

"You're a man, you wouldn't. She's got those big things out in front of her, and that's all a man notices. She doesn't even wear a brassiere. I can tell."

"I wish I could. I'll look more carefully the next time I see her."

"Oh, Harry."

"Are we going to argue?"

"If you want to."

"You were gone a long time."

"I apologized for that."

"I know you did."

"I didn't like the way she was looking at you," Grace said. "I didn't like it at all. She's been married twice."

"I know that. But what has that to do with it."

"She sleeps around."

"I've heard that. But, still, what has that to do with it?"

"I don't want you sleeping with her."

He tried to smile. "There's only one woman I want to 'sleep with,' as you put it, at the present time, and I don't seem to be getting very far with her."

"You will."

"When?"

"When the time is right."

"Oh, balls," he said.

"Don't say that."

"Why not?"

"I don't like it, that's all. It—it's vulgar. Besides, these people are friends of mine. I've known most of them since I was a little girl. I wouldn't want to be embarrassed."

"It's a common word, in common usage. I think it's mildly expressive of a certain cavalier viewpoint. Though in this case, to express my feelings more accurately, I could say, 'Crap.' " He spoke a little louder than before.

Few paid attention. A couple on the floor near the fieldstone fireplace turned and smiled and then went back to their chess game.

"See?" he said.

"I don't like you very much tonight, Harry."

"That's too bad. I was hoping—"

"I know what you were hoping. But it won't do you any good." She waved a hand in the air. "She got you all heated up, pushing those big things—"

"Yours aren't so small."

"—things in your face, and now you want to take it out on me."

"I don't want to take it 'out' on you. I want to—"

"Oh, go to hell!"

"Bye-bye," he said, rising to his feet.

"Harry?"

"I'm leaving. This party bores me. You bore me." He gulped down the remainder of his drink. "The whole god-damned thing bores me."

"Harry," she said, and stood beside him.

"It's a great life," he said.

"We're not making much of it."

"I'm not making much of anyone."

"You twist everything I say, twist it into something about sex. Why?"

"It's the way I am. I have a dirty mind."

"Let's get some air, Harry."

They went outside. The swimming pool was lit up by rose-colored lights and there were four or five people swimming. Harry saw John Ross and Bess sitting off to one side, near some rose bushes. He turned Grace the other way, found chairs in the shadows, and sat down.

She was quiet, waiting for him to speak. Actually, she was quite angry with herself for having let herself be drawn into the present situation. But when she had re-turned from the bathroom and seen them—Harry and Bess—sitting there, something had happened inside her. She had never been jealous in her life.

"I guess someone owes someone else an apology," she said.

"I guess so," he said.

They sat there. A big man with a potted stomach did a dive off the diving board; the water made a huge splash, almost reaching them in their seats.

"I apologize," she said.

"Fine."

"You could, too."

"I could, but I won't."

"Sometimes—" she started, but didn't finish it.

"Sometimes what?"

"I don't know."

"If you don't, I don't, either."

"What's wrong tonight, Harry?"

"Grace, we've known each other one week."

"That's enough for me. And besides, this is our third date."

He laughed. "That's a funny word—'date.' I picture a pair of teen-agers holding hands in the back row of a movie balcony, not a couple of old-timers like us."

"I'm not old. I'm twenty-five."

"That's old."

"How old are you?"

"Very, very old—thirty-two."

She smiled. "I was hoping it would be that."

"Why?"

"Well, if you ask me that, I can't really tell you why, not exactly. Maybe I saw a movie once or read it in a book or someone told it to me. I don't know. Anyway, it's seven years difference. It sounds nice."

"We're not arguing any more."

"No. You know, I can't imagine you as a teen-ager."

"I can't imagine myself as a teen-ager."

"Were you in the army?"

"Every stupid son of a bitch in the world was in the army. It's a thing you had to do. They just point a finger at you and say come on in, you dumb bastard, and there you are and you don't have a chance."

"Were you an officer?"

He laughed.

"Is that what you did when you were a teen-ager?" she asked.

"You mean hold hands?"

"Yes."

"That, and more," Harry said. "I always wanted to do more. I guess that's the way I am. I want to do more now, with you."

"I know you do. I've known that all along."

"I don't see how you could help but know it. I've said it often enough."

"Do you always do it with the girls you go out with?"

"Almost always. There have been exceptions. You're an exception. We've been out twice before, and nothing's happened yet."

"I think a lot has happened."

"Such as?"

"I'm falling in love with you."

"Oh, Jesus," he said.

"Does it sound trite?"

"It sounds worse than that. Much worse."

"Well, I am."

"Well, don't."

"How can you stop a thing like that?"

"You can."

"How?"

"You can grow up a little."

"I am grown up."

"Oh, Jesus," he said again.

"Quit saying that."

"Okay."

"That's the first time you've agreed with me tonight."

"Hurray for our side."

"Oh, cut it out, Harry."

"Well?"

"Well what?"

"How about tonight?"

"Just like that?"

"Just like that," he said.

They were interrupted by the approach of three people. He recognized them, having met them earlier, as Jack Perkins, Maria Nevarez and Carl Morris.

Perkins was a tall thin man with busy eyebrows and a receding hairline and a tendency to smile too much. He smiled now, and said, "You two look as if you've been having quite a conversation."

"We have been," Harry said.

"I can guess the subject," Morris said.

"You probably could," Harry said.

Maria said, "Do you like our town, Mr. Mercer?"

"It's like other towns," he said.

"A very cynical attitude," Perkins said, and smiled.

"Well, I've always been known as a rather cynical bastard, especially after the fourth drink, and I've had five tonight. At least, I think it's five. At any rate, my cynicism has been acquired over the years and there's not one thing I can do about it."

"I know one thing," Grace said. "You could be a little more polite."

"Well, I didn't know that politeness had anything to do with cynicism. What do you think of that, Mr. Morris?"

Morris looked bored and said, "I don't think anything of it."

Perkins, still smiling, said, "I understand you've worked in Europe for some years, Mr. Mercer."

"Your understanding is correct."

"Paris?"

"I've been there, yes."

"What's it like?"

"The same as Beach City."

Perkins passed cigarettes around. Morris flicked a a wooden match between his thumb and forefinger, holding the light for all of them.

"Come now, Mr. Mercer," Perkins said, "you must be pulling our legs."

"I thought 'pulling our legs' was an English expression," Harry said.

"It may be, at that," Maria said, and laughed.

"You're not English, are you, Mr. Perkins?" Harry asked.

He was looking at Maria Nevarez and liking what he saw. She had beautiful skin and deep, dark eyes and the blackest hair imaginable, pulled into a bun at the nape of her neck.

"No, I'm strictly Beach City, Mr. Mercer," Perkins said. "About Paris, I hear the women there are very nice."

"They are. Yes, they are."

Maria reminded him of a bullfighter's sister he had known in Madrid; it was a nice memory.

"Are they really—well, so different there?"

"They're smaller, Mr. Perkins."

"What do you mean, smaller?"

"What do you think I would mean?"

"I haven't the faintest idea."

"Then you'd better get your goddamned nose out of the gutter and find out what I mean."

"Harry!" Grace said.

Cynthia Ross came up then. "I'm sorry I've been neglecting you," she said, "but we've been having the most divine conversation in the other room about Dylan Thomas."

Grace said, "It's a nice party, Cynthia."

"I hope so. I hope everyone is having a nice time."

Harry did not like her. He did not know just why, but there had been something when the introductions had been made earlier in the evening, and whatever that something had been, it was still there. She was attractive, tall and slim, looking like an advertisement out of one of the women's magazines, but he still did not like her. She wore far too much makeup; her mouth looked grotesque.

"We're having a nice time," Grace said.

"It looks like it," said Morris.

"I like your husband, Mrs. Ross," Harry said.

"That's nice," Cynthia said. "John is a very nice man."

Morris laughed.

"How would you like a punch in the nose?" Harry asked.

"What?" asked Morris, surprised.

"I said, how—"

"Stop it, Harry!" said Grace.

"I don't like him," said Harry.

Morris tried to laugh again. Grace looked angry, while

Cynthia looked around at her other guests. Perkins had turned his back. Maria was looking at Harry, smiling broadly; she had nice teeth. She certainly reminded him of that bullfighter's sister.

Harry got to his feet. "I think we'd better be going."

"So early?" asked Morris.

"I'm a working man."

"Oh?" said Morris. "What do you do?"

"He's something at the paper," said Cynthia.

"Something is right," said Harry. He turned to Grace. "Are you coming with me?"

"I came with you, I'll go with you."

He saw Bess Higgins raise a hand to him as he left with Grace. He nodded in return.

He drove Grace home to the cottage on the beach at the south end of town. The cottage could not have come out of her teacher's salary, and he wondered how she had afforded it, then thought probably her family had been well-to-do. He parked the car in her driveway behind her own car, and listened to the sounds of the Pacific Ocean. They were good sounds, if you liked that sort of thing, and he did.

"Well," she said, turning to face him, her knees drawn up on the seat between them, "we certainly got out of there in a hurry."

"I guess we did."

"Do you always want to punch someone in the nose?"

"Not always. I just didn't like any of them. I didn't like Carl Morris. And I didn't like that Cynthia Ross in particular."

"That was quite obvious. She's my oldest and dearest friend. We went through school together."

"That doesn't mean anything."

"It does to me."

"May I come in?"

She hesitated. "No."

"Okay," he said.

"You can kiss me if you want."

"That'd be great!"

"Harry, what's wrong with you? You told me earlier to grow up a little. Maybe you should grow up a little, yourself. You've been acting like a spoiled child all night, and I don't like it one bit. You were very insulting to my friends. I can't understand you. You make no effort to have people like you."

"I don't give a damn what people think."

"Oh, come off it, Harry! You're talking like a college sophomore, not like an adult. You go around with your nose stuck in the air and think you're so damn much better than anyone else, but you're not, you're really not."

"Is this lecture night?"

"What do you want me to say, Harry? I saw you for the first time a week ago yesterday, Friday, and I flipped then and I'm still flipping. I know the biggest thing in your mind now is to get in bed with me, and I want that, too. God, you can't know how much I want that. But there are other things, other considerations, and you should think about them. Life isn't one big tussle in bed. It will come in time, and a lot more will come with it. I'm sure of that or I wouldn't be wasting my time with you."

"Grace, I think you may be jumping in without looking."

"What do you mean by that?"

"I mean you have something in mind."

"Of course, I have."

"I haven't."

"You will have, eventually. I'll see to that."

"You don't know anything about me, and yet you're virtually proposing to me."

"I'm not proposing to you, Harry. You'll do that, when

the time is right. But I know enough about you; I know enough for me."

"I could be divorced, and you could be a Catholic."

"I'm not a Catholic. Are you?"

"Am I what?"

"Divorced."

"No."

"So that's out of the way. It wouldn't make any difference, anyway."

"There are a lot of other things."

"We'll get them out of the way as we come to them."

"Jesus," he said, "you really mean it, don't you?"

"Of course I mean it. I've meant it all along. You're you, Harry Mercer, and I'm me, Grace Wallace, and nothing else matters."

He heard the distant sound of a fog horn. He wondered about that; it wasn't foggy.

He said, "A lot else matters."

"What? Name me something."

He smiled. "For one thing, I don't like your best friend. She gives me a pain in the butt. For another thing, I like the words I use and my language embarrasses you in front of your friends and I wouldn't want to go through life embarrassing you in front of your friends."

"You could learn other words."

"I could, but I wouldn't."

"You're very stubborn, Harry."

"That could be another thing."

"Harry, don't be like this."

"I'm being like myself."

"You weren't like this Tuesday night, when we drove to Los Angeles and went to the Bowl."

"Well, that was different. We were listening to Mozart."

"Thursday night then?"

"What did we do Thursday night?"

"Damn you, you remember. We had dinner at the Flamingo and then just talked, talked about writers and writing and life."

"Yes, I remember. You had some good ideas and I was properly impressed. You like Hemingway and O'Hara, don't you?"

"I think O'Hara is vulgar."

"All right, may I come in?"

"The answer is still no."

"You won't get me this way."

"I'll get you, Harry."

"The hell you will," he said,

She got out of the car and the first thing he thought of as he watched her walk across to her cottage was Bess Higgins.

It was a good thought.

John Ross sat on the edge of one of the twin beds in his underwear, wondering what he would say to her when she finally came into their room. What could he say? His head was a little fuzzy, but not too bad, considering. He had carefully counted his drinks during the course of the night, a habit he had gotten into the last few months; he had had eleven. He could remember when he would have had twice that number and felt no worse than he was feeling now. He smacked his lips.

He was only thirty-six, and yet tonight, at this moment, he felt much more than that. He looked down at himself, at the roll of fat around his middle, and wondered what had happened to him. Cynthia was only twenty-five. What had he been doing when he was only twenty-five? That would have been 1946. Was that the year he had traveled through Europe with his mother? No, that couldn't be, because the war had still been going on in 1946. Or had it? He couldn't really remember. He had not been in the war. His mother had had a friend who was on the draft board and he had never had the courage to enlist. He had wanted to go, really, but then his mother would have been all alone and he had not wanted that.

Cynthia came into the room.

"All the dogs gone home?" he asked.

She didn't answer.

He whistled a tune.

She still didn't answer.

He said, "It was a nice party."

She was in front of her dresser, removing her jewelry.

"Don't give me that crap," she said. "It was a lousy party, and you know it."

"Okay, so it was a lousy party."

She turned to look at him. "Are you drunk?"

"Of course I'm not drunk."

She came over to stand before him, turning her back to him. He automatically reached up, unzipping her zipper. She stepped neatly out of the dress, picked it up and went across to hang it in her closet. She was wearing stockings, a panty-girdle and a brassiere. Her body was deeply tanned.

He looked and wanted.

"Don't look at me like that," she said.

"That's all I do any more," he said. "Look."

"You know what I said."

"I couldn't do that, Cynthia."

"I don't know why not. Everyone else does."

"Who's everyone else?"

"Oh, for Chrisakes, quit grilling me!"

"I just wanted to know."

"Carl Morris, for one."

"Yes, I imagined that."

"You imagined right."

"Did he do it to you tonight? Did he?"

She removed her brassiere and rubbed her hands across her breasts. They were small, but high, with large nipples, and the memory of other times came to him and made him want her even more.

"Jesus," he said, "don't do that."

"Does it make you hot?"

"You know damned well it does."

"Then do something about it, John."

"That answers my previous question."

"What question?"

"About Carl Morris. He didn't do it to you tonight and no one else did, either, or you wouldn't be asking me."

"All right," she said.

She sat down on the twin bed next to his, removing her stockings and panty-girdle. She let him see her. She spread her legs so he would have a good look, and she smiled.

"Goddamn you," he said.

"You'll want it enough one of these nights."

"Never for that."

"You're kidding yourself, John."

"No, you're the one who's kidding yourself."

"It's not so bad, really. You should try it. You'll be too old one of these days and then that's all you'll be able to do."

"Did you ever—try it?"

"Of course I have."

"With whom?"

"That's none of your business. With more than one. You can know that."

"Grace?"

"Don't be absurd. Grace is quite normal, not at all like me. I wouldn't be the least bit surprised if she's still a virgin."

"She won't be long," he said, "not with that Harry Mercer. I liked him."

"I thought he was a perfect son of a bitch."

"You would. He didn't fall all over himself being nice to you."

"No, I know that. I saw him with Bess for a time."
She lay back on the bed, sighing deeply, and ran a hand
down the inside of one of her thighs. "I saw you with her,
too. Are you getting any from her, John?"

"I would if I could. I'd get it any place I could, don't
worry yourself about that."

"I know you would." She laughed. "When was the last
time, John?"

"With you?"

"With me."

"Five months ago."

"My, you do have strength of a sort. I didn't think
you'd last this long. I really didn't think you would."

"One of these nights, I'll take you by force."

She turned her head to look at him. "You couldn't. I'd
kill you first."

"I think you would."

"You know damned good and well I would."

"I have some rights, Cynthia."

"Don't give me that crappy line about a husband, and
all. I'm not an animal you bought to play with. I told
you what you had to do and you won't do that, so to hell
with you."

"I wonder why I ever married you."

"Because I was a hot piece then and you liked it and
I made you like it, that's why. You couldn't do without it
then, and you're not going to be able to do without it now.
You'll come around."

He told her what she could do.

She laughed. "That would solve most of the problems
of the world if one could do it."

She got up and went into the bathroom, closing the
door behind her. He heard the water running in the
shower.

He sat there and thought about it all. In the beginning,
she had been so damned exciting. She had let him do it
in the office one day, while she had been working for

him as a typist, and then once again, and then he could not stay away from her. His mother had been against the marriage; she had died a year later, still bitter against Cynthia, and now he could see his mother's point. Marrying Cynthia had been one of the few things he had ever done against his mother's wishes, and now he had only himself to blame. But how could he—or anyone—have known it would turn out like this? Lately, he had been thinking about suicide; the thought came to him more and more. But that would be giving her what she wanted, and he did not like that. His life had been wasted. His father had had the Lincoln-Mercury franchise before him, and had been smart enough to invest in real estate, so he had no money worries and never had had. He had been a pretty fair tennis player, good enough to win a few trophies, and that had been about all he had done with his life. Oh, he went to the office every day in the week, but the agency was really run by the sales manager, and he knew it, and he knew that everyone else knew it, too. They all laughed behind his back, but he did not mind that. As a matter of fact, he did not mind much of anything. He was alive and that was just about all. He played eighteen holes of golf twice a week and, lately, since Cynthia had put up those ridiculous standards for their sex life, he had been driving to Los Angeles once a week.

Cynthia came from the bathroom, rubbing herself with a huge orange turkish towel. There was a smile on her face and he hated her more then than he had ever loved her.

"Your turn," she said.

"I hate you," he said.

She laughed.

"Cynthia, we can't go on like this."

"Divorce me, then. That's all right with me."

"I know it would be. You'd have what you wanted."

"I have it now."

She lay back on her bed, spreading her legs again so that he could see her. She touched herself with her right hand, and her mouth was smiling as she looked at him.

"Take a cold shower, John. It'll do you good."

She was laughing when he got up and stamped into the bathroom, slamming the door after him. She heard the lock click and she laughed some more. She had him where she wanted him, and they both knew it. She would never give in, regardless. She had a right to her own choice, and she had made that choice; and if he didn't like that, he was perfectly welcome to go elsewhere. Dimly, she wondered if he did go elsewhere. That, she had to admit, was a possibility.

In the beginning, before their marriage and right at the start of it, she had allowed him to have his passion, and he had surprised her with the amount of that passion. There had even been a few times when she had enjoyed that, but they were few and far between. But that was all in the past now, and she did not have to think about it any more. No, she had her own life now, and he was not included in that life. She had what she wanted: a home, a respectable front, security, enough money to give her little parties and help sponsor the Beach Playhouse. Even if he divorced her, she would still have everything but the respectable front, and that didn't matter much any more, anyway. There was the community property law in California, and even half of John's money would suffice. She had planned this kind of life almost since her first breath, and now that she had it, she was extremely happy. Only tonight, thinking back on the party, she was not too happy.

Things hadn't gone right since the beginning of the evening. Carl Morris had arrived without Frank Manning and he had told her for sure that Manning would come tonight. She had been angry at Carl all evening for that. She had so looked forward to meeting Frank Manning; Carl had told her all about him, what he liked to do, and she had been looking forward to doing it with a celebrity like Frank Manning. She could imagine what she would feel, after having done it with him, to see him on the screen, knowing what she knew. And then that lousy bastard of a Jack Perkins had brought that little Mexican whore with him, that Maria Nevarez. She did not give a damn if the Nevarezes went all the way back to the beginnings of Beach City, or mankind, or what; Maria Nevarez was a whore and a Mexican—she remembered the time Maria Nevarez had laughed in her face—and if you let a Mexican in your house, you might as well let in a nigger, and then where would you be? Goddamn Jack Perkins. Goddamn Maria Nevarez. And then Grace— Grace, of all people!—had brought that perfect son of a bitch of a Harry Mercer with her. And who was Harry Mercer? Of all the goddamned gall, bringing a flunky newspaperman to one of her parties! She would have to speak to Grace about that. And, suddenly, Cynthia remembered the way Grace had looked at him, the way they had stayed aloof from the rest of the people, and that told her all she wanted to know. It had all been there, on Grace's face. Cynthia had known that when Grace eventually fell—and fall she would—it would be hard; Grace was that kind of a person. And now Cynthia was sure that Grace had fallen, and Cynthia pitied her; or, at least, felt as close to pity as was possible with her, for actually she had nothing within her to feel any kind of emotion—other than the only true one—and she knew this. But, after all, Grace was an old friend, a friend who had known her when, and so she supposed she should feel something for Grace.

Cynthia got up and went across to turn out the lights. She listened at the bathroom door, but heard nothing. She went back and pulled down the blankets on her bed and lay down, naked; she always slept that way. She rubbed her breasts and then her stomach and then farther down, and she was very disappointed at the way the night had turned out. She should not have been so angry at Carl

Morris. He would have done what she wanted, and then she wouldn't be feeling this—this anxiety. Damn all men. She could not really bring herself to do without them, for after all, for the most part, they would do what she wanted, and then she did not have to keep running after women all the time; but, still, she—

She heard him coming out of the bathroom, then the sound he made getting into bed. He sighed.

"It's not so bad, really, John."

"I told you what you could do."

"I bet you wish you could do that."

"Yes, I do."

"Come on, John. Try it. Just once."

He was silent.

She was a long time getting to sleep. She heard him breathing heavily long before she fell off.

Harry had stopped at a phone booth, looked up Bess Higgins's number, and had phoned her. No answer. He stopped at the first decent-looking bar he came to, had a drink and then another, and then, without calling, drove to her place. Just as he stopped, he saw a car pull into Bess's driveway. He saw her get out and enter the house and then the lights went on. He smoked a cigarette and then got out and went up to the front door. She answered his ring immediately. She still wore the dress she had worn at the party, but she had kicked off her shoes and was in her stocking feet.

"I've been expecting you," she said.

"I'm here."

The living room was medium-modern, nothing extreme other than a sort of cone-shaped ceramic piece on the mantelpiece. He noted the tray on the coffee table and the two drinks on it.

"You were expecting me," he said.

"Of course," she said. "I said that, didn't I? Take your

coat and tie off. I hate to be alone with a man with his coat and tie on. It's almost obscene."

He took his coat and tie off, and his shoes, and then took the drink she handed him and slumped down on the couch. She sat opposite him in a chair.

She said, "I knew you'd come around, Harry, dear. I've known Grace Wallace for almost ten years, ever since she was a snotty little kid with braces on her teeth. I know what kind of woman she is. I told you before, you wouldn't get any from her this night."

"What kind of woman is she?"

"You really want to know?"

"I guess not."

"I thought not."

He was staring up at the ceramic.

"Don't stare too long," she said. "I have a lot of time on my hands and that's my one vice. People pay money for them."

"Did you do that?"

"Yes."

"It's nice."

"Remember what I said about that word, Harry, dear. It's over-used. You can say what you really think. I understand you did that at the party."

"It's a phallic symbol."

She laughed. "Oh, no! Don't say things like that. I'm a normal one hundred percent woman and I have the memories of two husbands and maybe several other men to prove that, and I don't have to have things around the house to remind me of what I want. Let's not get into any conversation about phallic symbols. Talk like that bores me, and I don't want to be bored by you and—"

"Don't you?"

"—and besides, I get all that kind of talk I need at Cynthia's parties."

"Is that what goes on up there?"

"That, and more. Cynthia read a book one time and

she's a graduate of the state college and so she considers herself the leading artistic light of Beach City. You must know the type, and she is a type. I don't give a damn for art of any kind."

"But you do these ceramic pieces."

"The way I do them, it's not art."

"I'll bet it's an art the way you do something else."

"Don't rush things, Harry dear. I'm not sure just what I'm going to do with you. I'm going to sit here and listen to you and look at your face, and then I'll decide. Grace said no, and now you're here and I'm a woman and you want to toss me on the floor or the bed, whichever is quicker, and do what you wanted to do to Grace."

"That's possible."

"I know it's possible, Harry dear. It's more than possible. It's happened to me before. She used to go with Ramon Nevarez, Maria's brother, and he had to come around and talk to me later, the way you're doing."

"That Maria is something," he said.

"Yes, she is something. If I were a man and I had my choice of any woman in Beach City, I'd take Maria Nevarez."

"You're something, Bess."

"I know I'm something, Harry dear. You may find out, you may not."

"Don't you like Grace?"

"God help her, of course I like her. She's just mixed up, that's all, living in the wrong age or the wrong climate or something. She's a sweet kid."

"She said something like that about you."

"Yes, I can imagine."

"She said you didn't wear a brassiere."

"Harry, dear," she said, "you're pushing it. Don't. I'll let you know whether or not I wear a brassiere at the proper time. You'll find out, one way or the other."

He sat there and looked at her and wondered what in hell he was doing there.

"Harry, dear," she said, smiling, "don't sit there and think about everything. Concentrate on one thing. You fascinate me, Harry, and I'm not easily fascinated. You go out of your way to make trouble and I know you're not like that. I'm wondering why you act the way you do."

"Maybe because I'm pure bastard," he said.

"Maybe because you want people to think that. Have you ever been hurt, Harry, dear?"

"Good God no! Don't go romantic on me."

"You're sweet, Harry, dear."

"You're nuts."

"Of course, I'm nuts. I'm sitting here, looking at you and wanting you, wanting your goddamned hands on my body, and I'm talking about another woman, so I must be nuts. You don't have to tell me that."

She reached up and undid the top of her dress, allowed it to fall to her waist. Her breasts were bared, and she passed a hand across her nipples. She smiled and said, "Grace was right."

"I can see she was," he said, "in that instance."

She got up and left the room and, presently, he got up and followed her. She was in the bedroom, the pale light from the bedside lamp casting shadows on her naked body. She was still smiling, and she said, "Like what you see?"

"Looks okay from here," he said.

"Goddamn you," she said, "hurry up!"

"I'm not sure I want it," he said, and laughed.

She said, "You are pure, hundred percent bastard, Harry."

The first time was too quick as he had known it would be after all his drinking; and then the second time was much better and he knew what she was and she knew what he was and they lay back and switched off the lamp and were quiet in the darkness.

"God-Almighty-damn," she said, after awhile. "I never knew—I honestly never knew . . ."

"What did you expect?"

"Not that—that five-star production."

He put his head down and kissed one of her breasts gently.

"Get away from me," she said.

He laughed.

"Harry Mercer," she said, "I saw you come in with Grace tonight and I said to myself I've got to get in bed with that man or I'll die, I'll honestly die, and goddamn you, you're as good as you look."

"You would have made a great whore, Bess."

"Go to sleep," she said.

"There'll be more."

"Oh, my God, no! Not tonight. I hurt all the way up to my ears."

"I thought you were better than that."

"Oh, you brute! You lousy brute, you!"

"Is that what I am?"

"You know what you are."

"I know, I know."

"That goddamned lucky Grace Wallace."

"Why do you say that?"

"She'll be getting you all the time. She doesn't know how lucky she is."

He turned over on his side and went to sleep.

three

GRACE WALLACE saw him, his feet resting on the desk, ankles crossed, his hands clasped behind his head, his eyes half-closed. She paused in the doorway looking at him for a long moment before she said, "Good morning, Harry."

He opened his eyes fully, but made no other movement.

"What are you doing here?" he asked.

Without answering, she walked across the room, leaned against the edge of his desk and looked around. She had never been in a newspaper office before, and she was a little awed. She had seen them, re-created in the movies and on television, and there had always been a great deal of hustle and bustle and general excitement. Now, there was nothing, nothing but a big empty room with cluttered desks and silent typewriters, and a lonely man sitting with his feet propped up on the desk.

"Is it always like this?" she asked.

"Always like this on a Sunday morning. There's nothing so peaceful as a newspaper office on a Sunday morning. I like it. Nothing to bother you, no one to interfere, just quiet. It's almost like a library, without the disadvantage of having people around."

"It's rather frightening," she said.

Harry ignored her.

She saw the half-empty container of coffee. She picked it up, took a sip; it was cold. He would have been here a long time, sitting alone.

"Did you have breakfast?" she asked.

"Yes, Grace, I had breakfast."

"Are you working on a story?"

"No, Grace, I am not working on a story."

"This is what you like, isn't it? This aloneness, this being here in this big empty room, and then you don't have to put up the front that you put up, the front that I don't believe, and that you don't believe, either."

He was silent for a moment, then he said: Some day, if I ever have the time or the talent or maybe both, I'll write a book and I'll tell a story about a woman like you, Grace. It would make a good story, I think. Someone told me you were living in the wrong age or the wrong climate, or something like that, and I think I may agree. You should have lived when the marriages were arranged, and then you wouldn't have had to bother that pretty little head of yours. And you wouldn't be worrying me."

"Am I worrying you?"

"Of course you are."

"That's a good sign. I like that," she said.

"I don't," he said.

She noticed for the first time—and that surprised her, for she had thought she had memorized every detail of his appearance—the slight nick of a white scar above his right eyebrow. She put a hand out, touching the scar gently, and then withdrew her hand, almost as if she were afraid of hurting him.

"Where did you get that?"

"It's a long story."

"I have the time," she said.

"It isn't long anyway, not really," he said. "It was in Paris, the Palais de Sport, in forty-eight or forty-nine, I forget which. He was an Algerian with a lot of hair on his chest and arms, and I remember he had the damnedest eyes I ever saw; I can't explain those eyes, but I remember them, and they scared me. He knew I was scared and he pounded hell out of me for almost four rounds and I wouldn't go down and then he butted me with his head, and it was like a piece of granite or rock or something, and my head split open and the referee stopped the fight."

"I didn't know you had been a fighter," she said.

"I have been everything," he said, "but I wasn't a fighter."

"But you said—"

"I know what I said. But I still wasn't a fighter. I was scared to death. I was broke and I needed the money and I thought what the hell, he can't hurt me, and I was so damned wrong. He hurt me very much."

"I love you, Harry," she said.

He put his feet down on the floor and turned and looked at her once, and then away again.

"What time is it?" he asked.

"A little after eleven," she said.

"Shouldn't you be in church or something?"

"I don't go. Not very often."

He smiled. "I thought you were a good little Christian girl with good little Christian ideals."

"Don't make fun of me, Harry."

"I'm not, Grace. I'm really not."

"Kiss me, Harry."

He looked at her, and shook his head.

He searched his pockets for cigarettes, found an empty pack, crushed it, and tossed it at a waste basket, missing.

"The story of my life," he said.

"Is this feel-sorry-for-Harry-day?"

"Yes, this is feel-sorry-for-Harry-day. Sometimes I have to have days like this. I have a lot to feel sorry for myself for, and don't you think I don't."

"We all do, if we want it that way."

"Please, no philosophizing, not on Sunday."

"What's wrong, Harry?"

"With what?"

"With you, with us."

"Nothing's wrong with me. I'm just me, that's all. There's a lot of things wrong with us, too many things to talk about, and you should know that. You, of all people, should know that."

"Do you want me to go, Harry?"

"No, I don't want you to go, Grace. I'm a coward, and I don't want you to go. I want you to stand there, leaning up against this desk so that I can look at you and think about you and wonder about what might have been. And I don't want you to go."

"Has there ever been a woman, Harry?"

"There have been women," he said.

"That's not what I asked you," she said.

"I know what you asked me, and I gave you your answer, but I'll spell it out for you. Why is it that all women want to know the answer to that question? It's uncanny. It's almost a stock question. I think maybe you and all women like you read the wrong book or saw the wrong movie when you were growing up, and now each and every man has to have had a great lost love, someone he's been pining away for over countless years. No, Grace, there's never been 'a woman' and there never will be 'a woman.' I have neither the time nor the inclination for 'a woman' and don't ask me why because I don't know and even if I did I wouldn't tell you why. No, that's not quite right, either. There was 'a woman' one time, and I thought she was the most beautiful thing that ever existed—sensitive-looking, intelligent-looking, sensuous-looking—everything a man would want, and I loved her from a great, great distance and then she did something that was very wrong according to our society and I found myself condemning her like the rest of the herd, even though I didn't want to condemn her and I didn't know the circumstances. She could have been perfectly right in what she did, and I didn't know, I just went along with the rest and branded her, and I myself destroyed that love I had had for her, because of the way I felt she should have acted, yet I didn't know one damn thing about it, anyway. Her name was Ingrid Bergman."

"Harry you're very bitter."

They both laughed.

"Yes, Grace, I'm bitter."

"You're very bitter and you feel sorry for yourself and I wonder what I see in you."

"You see in me someone new, someone you haven't seen before, someone who doesn't conform to your way of thinking, and you believe you can change me, make me think the way you do. You're very much wrong, Grace, very much wrong. You would see that in time."

She shook her head. She moved away from the desk, walking toward the glassed-in room at the rear. She stood there, looking through the glass, and then asked: "What are those?"

He said, "That's the Associated Press room, and those are teletype machines. The news from all over the world comes in on those machines, gathered by hard-working little men in all of the out-of-the-way places of the world, trying to tell the rest of the world what is going on, and you get it here in Beach City. Then some damned fool pencils out what he doesn't like, and you get two or three short paragraphs to read when and if you have time and you probably don't read it, anyway. And so you don't know what's going on in the world and you don't give a damn anyway, so what difference does it make? What difference does it make if some poor little bastard in Greece has watered soup once a day and that's all, and what difference does it make if some poor slob in Lower Slobbovia stands up on his toes and tells some other poor slob to go to hell and let him do what he wants and gets shot in the guts for it, and what difference does it—"

"Cut it out, Harry!"

"Sure, you're mad now, aren't you? You're mad because I'm telling the truth and no matter how trite it sounds, the truth hurts. You'd rather read about some goddamned movie star getting screwed in the back row of a movie house or son of a bitch chopping up his wife and kids with a meat ax."

"I'm not mad, Harry. That's the way things are, and I don't think there's much we can do about it. You're using it as an excuse right now, hoping that I'll believe you feel all these things, only I know you don't, Harry."

"That's a good answer," he said.

She came back to lean against the desk again. She looked down into his face, and smiled, and she saw what she wanted to see there, and she smiled again.

She said, "I thought this was Sunday and there was to be no philosophizing."

"I got out of hand," he said.

He put a finger up, quite suddenly, touching her face.

"I spent the night with Bess Higgins."

"I imagined you did," she said.

"You're sweet, Grace. Bess said that about you, and I'm saying it, too. I don't know exactly what sweet means, but that's what you are, Grace, and whenever I think about you I'll think what a sweet person you are, and then I'll be happy and I'll know you're happy, too. You're sweet, Grace."

She laughed, nervously; she didn't know why; it was something she couldn't control.

"I'll see you this afternoon," she said. "Around three."

"What?"

"Remember? We have a date. A picnic on the beach at my place. You and I and Maria and Jack."

"You want me to come?"

"Of course I want you to come."

"You're sweet, Grace."

"I'll leave you now. You put your feet back up on the desk, Harry, and you sit here and think your thoughts and damn the whole world and nurture your bitterness a little and feel sorry for yourself a little, and then I'll see you at three o'clock, and everything will be better."

"Will it, Grace?"

"I'm sure it will, Harry."

She leaned down, kissing him on the cheek. "I still love you," she said.

She left him like that, alone, with his feet back up on the desk, with his eyes half-closed.

Harry stood digging his toes into the warm sand, watching the distant sailboats lean this way and that, listening to the music coming from the cottage behind him.

The screen door slammed, and he turned and saw her coming down the three steps into the sand. She wore a one-piece black bathing suit, and she was long-legged, high-breasted and deeply tanned. Her mouth smiled as she came up to him, and he did not like anything about it, not anything at all.

"What's that?" he asked.

"What's what?"

"That music."

"Oh, *An American in Paris*—Gershwin."

"Yes, I know. Gershwin."

"Maria and Jack are late."

"I hope they never come," he said.

"They will," she said.

"My God, Grace, you're beautiful!"

She looked up at him for a moment, and then put a forefinger against her lips and then that same forefinger against his lips.

"And you're cute, Mr. Mercer," she said.

They ran down to the beach together, holding hands. The coldness of the water was a sharp sting against his feet and ankles, and then a wave hit his thighs and he removed his hand from hers and dived into an incoming breaker, coming up sputtering and coughing from a lungful of salt water.

She was beside him, her mouth open in laughter, her hair flat and wet around her face, her very, very beautiful face, and he ducked underneath and caught her around her thighs and pulled her down.

They came up together. They swam around for another ten minutes, and then went in.

Jack Perkins and Maria Nevarez were sitting on a bright-colored blanket, smiling at them.

"Two beautiful creatures from the sea," Maria said.

"Thank you," Harry said.

"Thank you," Grace said.

"You are beautiful, Grace," Jack said, and laughed.

"Thank you again," Grace said. She laughed also.

The breeze was almost cold now. He wrapped himself in a towel and sat down on the edge of the blanket, close to Maria, looking at her.

"Have you ever been in Spain in March?" he asked.

She shook her head.

He said, "I'll trade you for the afternoon, Jack."

"Hey, there!" Grace said.

Maria laughed and ran a hand before her eyes. "You're in a much better humor today, Mr. Mercer, than when we saw you last night."

"Who's Mr. Mercer?" he asked.

"You are, Mr. Harry Mercer," Maria said. "The very distinguished reporter, Mr. Harry Mercer. The very distinguished foreign correspondent, Mr. Harry Mercer. The very distinguished gentleman, Mr. Harry Mercer. The very dis—"

"Don't forget the very distinguished prizefighter, Mr. Harry Mercer," said Grace.

"Okay," said Maria. "The very distinguished prizefighter, Mr. Harry Mercer. The very—"

"So he's distinguished," said Jack. "So you cut it out or I'll get jealous. And you know how I am when I'm jealous."

"How is he when he's jealous?" asked Harry.

"Oh, he's very mean," said Maria. "Very, very mean. He won't let me watch Groucho Marx when he's jealous."

"I'm a real mean man," said Jack.

Grace finished fluffing herself dry with a towel.

"I wish you had let me do that," said Harry.

"I was thinking the same thing," said Jack.

"Now I might get jealous," Marie said, "and you know how I am when I'm jealous."

"We're all being very mean and very jealous today," said Grace.

"I'm also being very hungry," said Harry. "When do we eat?"

"Ah, I'm disappointed in you, Mr. Harry Mercer," said Maria. "I go back to my own true love, my balding little banker who is so jealous all the time that he cannot think of food. I am back with you, Jack."

"That's good," said Jack.

"Help me, Maria," said Grace.

"I thought I was a guest," said Maria.

"Only the men are guests, the lucky fools," said Grace. The two women went inside.

Harry asked, "Aren't you going in for a swim?"

"Maybe later," Jack said.

They lit cigarettes, and sat there, watching the distant sailboats.

"I'm not a bad guy, Harry," Jack said.

"I know that, Jack."

"I was born and raised in Beach City and I spent the war behind a desk in San Francisco and was discharged a first lieutenant. Autobiography. I envy you, Harry."

"We'll get along, Jack."

"Be good to her, Harry."

He turned and looked at Jack Perkins, and then he smiled.

"I'm glad it wasn't me you wanted to poke in the nose last night," Jack said. "I would have taken you up on it, and then I would have been embarrassed as all hell, getting my nose punched."

"This is paradise," said Harry. "This little plot of land right here is paradise."

"You know why I envy you, Harry?"

"No."

"Neither do I. I wish I did."

"Let's get drunk together some night, Jack."

"I think it'd be a hell of a lot of fun."

"It would be that, all right, Jack."

Jack was silent for a moment, and then he flipped his

cigarette out across the sand, and said: "I think maybe I know one of the reasons why I envy you, Harry. You look like a guy who has done things and been places, and all my life I've wanted to do things and go places, but I'm Beach City Perkins, and so I have to sit on my dead ass in this dead town and try and learn how to run a bank. I'm not doing a very good job of that, either. I wasn't kidding last night, when I asked you about the women in Paris. I wish to hell I knew about the women in Paris, Harry. I love Maria and I'm going to marry her and I wouldn't have it any other way, but still I wish I knew about the women in Paris."

"You should know about the women in Madrid."

"What?"

"Private joke, Jack. Anyway, the women in Paris are the same as the women here."

"I don't doubt you, Harry. But you see, you can sit there and say that and know what you're talking about and I can't."

"Are you really going to marry Maria, Jack?"

"I most certainly am."

"I thoughts things weren't that way, here in Beach City. I thought there was a line that no one crossed."

"They can go screw themselves," Jack said.

"I think I like you, Jack."

"Well, I like myself, Harry."

The two women came back out, carrying a wicker basket of cold chicken sandwiches and potato salad, and a jar of dill pickles, and a jar of green olives, and red ripe tomatoes, and a dozen cans of ice-cold beer.

"Hell," Harry said, "I thought we were going to roast weiners or something."

"You'll eat cold chicken sandwiches and like it," said Maria.

"Besides," said Grace, "it's against the law to have a fire on the beach."

"Civilization spoils everything," said Harry.

"You are cynical, Mr. Harry Mercer," said Maria.

"Is it cynical not to like civilization?"

"It is in Beach City," said Jack. "There's a city ordinance against it."

"Then I guess I'd better change my tune," said Harry.

"I knew you would, sooner or later," said Grace.

They sat around the blanket and ate the food and drank cans of ice cold beer, and then got some more beer, and drank that, too.

"A regular orgy," said Harry.

"You're mis-using the word," said Grace.

"No, I'm not."

"I don't think he is," said Jack.

"A battle of the sexes," said Grace.

"An orgy pertains only to excessive sexual happenings," said Maria.

"What is a 'sexual happening?'" asked Harry.

"Oh, you two!" said Maria. "You should both have your heads dunked in the water."

"There's only one way to settle this," said Grace.

They waited, drinking more beer, while she went inside and then came back again, carrying a book.

She said, "For authority, I'm going to quote *Webster's New World Dictionary of the American Language.* 'The College dictionary containing the most modern and complete record of words and phrases, the fullest etymologies, and—'"

"What was that word again?" asked Maria.

"'—etymologies, and the most discriminative synonymies.'"

"What?" asked Jack.

"'Synonymies'", said Grace. "'Over one hundred forty-two thousand vocabulary entries. More than one thousand two hundred illustrations—'"

"Maybe they'll have an illustration of an orgy," said Harry.

" '—one thousand seven hundred and sixty pages. College edition.' "

"Let's make a small wager on this," said Jack.

"All right, what?" asked Grace.

"If Jack and I win," said Harry, "we get to do whatever we want to do for the rest of the day and night."

"Sounds fair," said Jack.

"Go to hell," said Grace.

"Likewise," said Maria.

"A kiss in the dark then," said Harry.

"Mr. Harry Mercer," said Maria, "I revise my original conception of you. You are not a gentleman. You are a high school boy, Mr. Harry Mercer."

"Do you accept the bet or not?" asked Harry.

"How dark does it have to be?" asked Grace.

"Dark dark," said Harry.

"I accept," said Grace.

"All right," said Maria.

"Okay," said Jack.

Grace said, "It's on page ten thirty-three and I quote: 'One. In ancient Greece and Rome, feasting and wild celebration in worship of certain gods. Two. Any wild, riotous merrymaking. Three. An overindulgence in any activity.' "

"Well," said Jack, "I can hardly wait until it gets dark."

"Dark dark remember," said Maria.

"You won't have long to wait," said Grace.

The others looked to where she was pointing. A huge mass of dark clouds had formed suddenly on the horizon, giving promise of a coming storm.

"You know, going back to orgy," said Jack. "I've always maintained that the male of the species was smarter than the female. This proves it."

"That's a fact, Jack," said Harry. "Look at Switzerland."

"What do you mean, Mr. Harry Mercer?"

"I mean the women in Switzerland haven't the right to

vote. And Switzerland has managed to stay out of wars since—well, I don't know, but it's been a very long time."

"Ever since that guy shot the apple off his son's head," said Jack.

"William Tell," said Grace.

"Good God, she's smart," said Harry.

"She's an exception to the rule," said Jack.

"I beg to disagree," said Grace. "You're both crazy."

"Okay," said Harry. "Let's analyze this thing carefully and with malice towards none. We'll take the arts. The arts are supposedly filled with intelligence. Name me a great woman painter to compare with Degas and Van Gogh and Goya or El Greco or—"

"Grandma Moses," said Grace.

"She's got us there," said Jack.

"A good point," said Harry. "We concede it. Let's go on. Name me a woman author to compare with Hemingway or Balzac or O'Hara or Dickens or Wolfe or—"

"Agatha Christie," said Maria.

"George Sand," said Grace.

"*Who* Sand?" asked Jack.

"*George* Sand," said Grace.

"I think she must be a ringer," said Jack. "Or even a spy. I accept Agatha Christie, but anyone with a name like George—I don't know."

"She smoked cigars," said Harry. "I don't think we can accept anyone who smoked cigars as a legitimate woman."

"She was French," said Grace.

"Ah, that explains it," said Jack.

"I'm bored," said Maria. "I wish it would get dark."

"Dark dark," said Grace.

"We don't have to wait," said Jack.

"A bet is a bet," said Harry.

"Do you realize that the way things are going, we might have a woman president one of these days?" asked Jack.

"I'd shoot myself," said Harry.

"I'd be glad to help you," Maria offered.

"Hell," said Harry, "on second thought, I guess a woman president wouldn't be so bad, after all. Think of what would happen if women got in control of General Motors or Standard Oil, Holy Jesus!"

"In that case," said Jack, "there would have to be some kind of biological change. Men would have to have the babies."

"How dull," said Maria.

"We'd better get inside anyway," said Grace. "That storm is coming up fast."

They gathered up the things and went inside. Almost as soon as they were in, the first huge drops of rain started spattering. The wind crushed against the glass windows facing the ocean. The small cottage shuddered before the sudden onslaught.

"We'd better go," Maria said.

"She can't wait for dark," said Harry.

"She's impatient that way," said Jack.

"I'm glad," said Harry.

They said their goodbyes, and Jack and Maria left.

Harry opened his eyes. It was completely dark, but he knew he was lying with his head resting in her lap. He could feel the soft coolness of her hand against his forehead. The rain was a steady, continuous thing now, and he enjoyed the sound of it, the only sound in the night. She had changed into capri pants and a brief halter and he could feel the beginning swell of her breasts against his face. He reached up his hand, touching her breast, and then dropped his hand.

"Nice," he said.

"Very nice," she said.

"The end of the world," he said.

He felt her moving, and then the brush of her lips

against his cheek, and then the sudden soft sound of her laughter.

"Your bet," said Grace. "I've paid off."

"Thanks."

He turned over on his side, crooking an arm around behind her head, pulling her face down to his. The kiss was long and sweet and then suddenly fierce and passionate, and then she pulled away. He dropped his hand, undoing the halter, and her bare breasts were against his face and he was kissing them and feeling them and he could hear the sounds coming from deep down inside her, and then her mouth was against his again and he tried to pull her down to lie beside him, and she fought against him.

"No, no, no, no," she said. "No."

"Grace."

"No, Harry."

He got up and searched for the light, found it, and turned it on. She was sitting on the couch, looking at him, her breasts still bared. She smiled a small smile, bent down to pick up her halter and put it on.

"Son of a bitch," he said.

"It's not easy, Harry," she said.

"No, Grace, I guess it isn't."

"I'm sorry, Harry."

"You should be, Grace. You should be very damn sorry."

"I just can't do it. Not without—"

"Not without what?"

"Love," she said.

"Do you want me to tell you I love you? Is that it?"

"I want you to mean it, Harry."

"I've never said that, Grace. I've never said that to any woman, and I never will say it. It's not worth the saying."

"Do you want some coffee?"

"No, I don't want any goddamned coffee."

"It was a nice day, Harry."

"It's a lousy night, Grace."

"Maybe you'd better go, Harry. I feel we're going to have a bad argument, and I don't want to have a bad argument. Not tonight."

He slammed the door on his way out.

four

HARRY sat in the lonely, darkened hotel room, trying to blot everything from his mind, trying desperately not to think of Grace, of her beauty, the lusty remembrance of his lips against her breasts, the touch of her mouth against his.

He wondered what was wrong with him, why he couldn't let himself go and become involved in a wholesome relationship with her.

He grinned crookedly. "Wholesome" was a funny word for someone like himself to be using. He was not accustomed to thinking such thoughts, thinking such words, and he knew that, slowly but surely, the net was being thrown around him, drawing him in, and that he would have to fight against it if he wanted to retain any part of his own personality, to be his own man. He had told himself long ago that he would never be so stupid as to be caught in the deadly day-by-day struggle, being the same as everyone else, conforming to the dull gray pattern of the masses. That was not for him, not any.

He would have to be careful. Very careful.

Grace was potent, strong-willed, intelligent and beautiful. She had everything going for her and, he thought, she had probably never tasted the bitterness of defeat. She would be the kind who would want something and

then go out and get it, regardless. She wanted him now, of
that there was no doubt; and this, he had to admit,
frightened him a little. He did not want the same things
in life that she wanted. He wanted freedom; he wanted
mobility and the opportunities to do what he wanted to
do when he wanted. There could be no life like that
with her. She would be harsh and uncompromising in
this.

He rose from the chair, stretching, feeling a slight
twinge of tiredness in the small of his back. It had been
such a wonderful day, this day, right up to the end.
He had enjoyed the swim and the picnic and the non-
sensical conversations with Jack and Maria. They were
both good people and he admired them for being what
they were; he had no illusions about them, knowing that
each fitted into a special little niche in the community of
Beach City. Yet they were doing their best to escape
those niches and that's all that anyone could possibly do.

The ringing of the telephone shattered the stillness in
the room. He stood a moment, silently debating whether
or not to answer it; he decided against it. The ringing
ceased after awhile and he sighed contentedly. He had an
idea that would have been Grace. She would not give up
easily and she would not want him to remain angry with
her.

He walked to the window, raising the blind and opening
the sash, letting in the cool night breeze. He sucked the
air into his lungs, and looked out at the blinking lights
of the town.

Sunday night. How many Sunday nights had he spent in
hotel rooms just like this one? How long would he continue to drift? But this was what he wanted; this was
what he had to have, a course that he had committed
himself to so long ago that he could not remember
the actual moment of decision. Perhaps it had been
during the war, that coldly vicious time when he had
been taught that life was meaningless when it belonged

to someone else. Or perhaps it had been before that, during high school, when his voluptuous Spanish teacher had taken him to her bed and taught him so many of the things that still remained with him. Perhaps it had been even before that, during the long talks he had had with his father, listening to the older man's cynicism and bitterness.

He turned from the window, suddenly angry. He did not like this soul-searching; it was not like him, and again he felt that net entangling him, pulling him ever so gently, trying to change him into something he could never be. Why did he allow himself the torture of self-doubts of himself and his intentions? Grace was beautiful, yes, with that wonderfully sensuous kind of body that God gave only to a chosen few. But—let's face it—that's all she was and all she could ever be, and he had seen beautiful and sensuous women before, many of them.

He could not get entangled with her. He enjoyed his life, the life he had picked out for himself and he would not change it, not for her.

He heard the slight knock at the door. He hesitated a moment. Could she be contrite enough to come to his room and apologize for her actions earlier? Or try to make amends? He felt the tiny knot of apprehension tighten in his stomach. He wanted Grace as much as he had ever wanted any woman, yet she always seemed just beyond his reach, as if he could continue grasping for her forever and never quite catch hold of her.

The knock came a second time.

He walked across and opened the door. The light from the hallway splashed into the room and he laughed as he saw Bess Higgins standing there, a puzzled look on her face.

"Well," she said, "that's the first time anyone's ever laughed at me before I opened my mouth."

"I'm sorry," he said. "I'm just glad to see you."

"That glad? You have to laugh like an idiot just because you see me?"

"Why not?"

"Okay." She shrugged. "Have it your way. Now, am I going to stand out here in the hall all night or are you going to ask me in? If you've got a blond stashed away in the bed, I can come back later."

"Come on in," he said, taking her by the arm, half-pulling her into the room, closing the door after her.

"My God, Harry," she said, "do you always sit around in the dark like this? For crying out loud, turn on some light in this place. The dark frightens me when I'm alone with a man, especially when the man's you."

He laughed again, not so loudly this time. He liked this woman; she was completely without pretense, and she had accepted him as he was, which pleased him. He flicked on the wall switch and a pale overhead light flooded the room with its sickly yellow glow.

"I think the dark's preferable to that," she said.

She walked across to a brass floor lamp set between the two easy chairs on one side of the room, switching on the light. He liked the way she walked, the easy motion of her whole body in movement, and he remembered their passion of the previous night, the ultimate glory of sharing this red-headed woman's body and he felt a sudden warm pulse start its throbbing.

She was looking straight at him when he turned back from switching off the overhead light, candid appraisal in her eyes. He noted for the first time that her eyes were a curious, off-shade green, a deep, intense color that was accentuated by the red of her hair. It was as if he had not really seen her before, and he was slightly surprised by this. He had pictured her as something like a big, blustery woman with a ravenous appetite for life, devouring everything in her way, grabbing at everything that came by, eager not to miss anything before the end of the ride.

Now, looking at her, he could see that she was not as large as he had thought. She was tall, yes, with a healthy solidity of big bones about her, but there was not an extra ounce of flesh on her, and the warmth of her eyes and mouth betrayed the kindness she tried to hide from the world.

"You know, Bess," he said slowly, "you're a damned good-looking woman."

She actually blushed, turning from him, and he was surprised at this. She shrugged out of her tan top coat and he saw that she was wearing a dark-brown tweed skirt, very full, and a gold-colored blouse; her large breasts taut against the restrictions of the blouse. She caught him staring at her and he could tell that she was flustered. She fumbled in her purse, stuck a cigarette in her mouth and lighted it, pushing the smoke in his direction.

"Cut it out," she said.

"Cut what out?"

"That. Standing there staring, looking right through me as if I had just stepped off the latest express from Mars or Venus. You've seen me before. Hell, you've seen everything I've got, Harry, so quit looking like that."

"I wasn't aware that I was looking at you in any special way," he said. "Perhaps a little hungrily."

She tried to laugh. "I suppose I should make up some excuse, that I was just passing by or I was in the neighborhood, or something. I called and you didn't answer the phone and I knew you were up here."

"How could you know?"

"I saw you come in the lobby an hour or so ago. I was in the bar with a friend, having a drink. You looked—you looked like hell, Harry, and I wanted to run over to you and hold you and tell you that nothing in this world is worth getting that upset about, nothing and no one.

"But I sat there on my fanny and had another drink and listened to this friend of mine talking about what a pure bastard her husband has turned out to be, and all the time I was thinking about you, that look you had on your face."

"You're quite a gal, Bess," he said.

"Sure I am. I'm the greatest, didn't you know?"

They stood quietly, looking at each other, Bess occasionally taking a puff on her cigarette, the smoke billowing out between them. The minutes ticked by and he felt a strange sensation, as if he were floating through air and there was no place he would ever be able to stop and get off. He was aware of her, of the soft, moist look of her lips, the way the lower lip stuck out invitingly, the bright shine in her eyes as she stared back at him, challenging him in anything he wanted to do. And he wanted to go to her and sweep her up in his arms and feel the crush of her body against his, hear the strident callings from deep in her throat. Yet he stood there, waiting, puzzled by his inability to move or to think beyond this one moment.

"We could always get a job in the waxworks," she said finally, "standing in for the dummies."

He laughed.

"That's a good sound," she said. "I like it."

He walked to the phone and asked room service to send up a bottle of bourbon and the fixings. Turning, he saw a slight change in her eyes.

"I feel like getting drunk," he said.

"Why?"

"Do I need a reason?"

"A man like you, Harry, needs neither rhyme nor reason. I told you before something about Grace, how I thought she was living in the wrong age. I think the same thing about you. You don't fit the twentieth century. I see you on the deck of a whaler, the salt spray lashing your face, the gale beating your ship, your men looking to you for courage and guidance. I see you in strange ports with strange women, tasting, experiencing, getting to know everything, roaming the high, wild seas."

She sighed, sinking into one of the chairs, a perplexed look on her face. "I guess," she went on, "I need a drink, too. After that speech, I surely need something."

"We understand each other, Bess."

"Do we?"

"I sure as hell hope so."

There was a knock at the door and he turned, opening it, letting the bellboy bring in the tray with the bottle, ice bucket and glasses. He tipped the bellboy, caught the latter's quick glance in Bess's direction as he left.

After he took his time mixing two drinks, he handed her one. She sipped at the glass, nodding, and then said, "Why didn't you answer the phone, Harry?"

"I didn't feel like it," he answered, sitting on the edge of the bed. Suddenly the room was too warm, too stuffy, and he felt himself breathing hard, searching for that next breath of air. This was the pattern of his life, the whole pattern that hadn't changed since the end of the war. A bottle, a hotel room, a woman—

"I'm a shameless hussy," she said, holding her drink before her, staring at it. "I have no pride and I admit it. Last night—well, I didn't want to think about last night. It was almost too good to be true. A woman like me searches around and she knows. Harry, it was good and it could become a habit, and I'm not sure either of us want that. I spent the day trying to block you out of my mind and I think I was succeeding until that moment I saw you walking across the lobby with that beat expression on your face. I know you were with Grace and I know she turned you down; I told you before, Harry, that she'll always turn you down until you say what she wants to hear. I'm not going to be around all the time and you can believe that. But I'm here now, with no strings attached, simply because you're a man and I'm a woman and we both know what to do with what we've got."

"You talk a lot."

"I sure do."

"You're still a damned good-looking woman."

"Am I really, Harry?"

"Don't get coy on me. You've heard it before."

"A woman never hears that kind of talk too often."

"Are you going to sit over there all night or are you going to come over here where it's more comfortable?"

"I thought you wanted to get drunk," she said.

"I changed my mind. Okay with you?"

She rose slowly, finished her drink and dropped her glass to the floor where it rolled along the carpeting. She stood there a moment staring at him, then came slowly toward him, her walk eloquently sensuous. He rose to meet her and everything else was blotted from his mind, everything but the extreme joy of holding this woman.

"Oh, Jesus!" she murmured between clenched teeth. "Harry, you're the best, the absolute best! Get me out of these clothes. Please, Harry!"

And his hands were fumbling with her clothes, almost tearing them off, the lust ripening within him, ready to burst forth. His hands went over her naked skin, smooth, silken and burning hot, and he was only dimly aware of her hands against him, undressing him, until that moment when they both fell on the bed, their bodies locked in a tight embrace, a tangle of arms and legs and mouths, seeking and finding. Then there was nothing else in the whole world but the continual climbing and reaching, higher and higher until he thought he would sail right through the ceiling, and then, in that last split second, the delicious agony of knowing it was ending as it should, together . . .

To Grace, the night seemed bitterly cold and empty. She stood in the sand before her cottage, listening to the remnants of the storm passing beyond the mountains behind Beach City. The wind whistled across the water, sending the white-capped waves into a pounding, foam-

ing frenzy. Away out beyond the breakwater, she cu ..
barely make out a light bobbing up and down, occasionally disappearing from her view. She wondered what hardy
soul would be out in weather like this.

She shuddered, feeling the cold deep within her, yet
forcing herself to remain there in the face of the wind,
almost as if she were trying to defy it, to prove that
she was as strong as it was. The wind flattened the
skin of her face, giving her a curiously exhilarating
feeling.

She wondered where he was, what he was doing, what
he was thinking about. Could he be thinking of her
as she was thinking of him? Was it possible for the
thoughts of two different minds to meet in the vacuum
of space?

She turned and stumbled, falling to her knees as a
sudden harsher gust of wind ripped at her clothing, almost
tearing it from her body. She rested there a moment to
gain strength, then rose and walked unsteadily to the
cottage. The door was almost torn from her grasp by
the strength of the wind. She pushed the door shut, leaned
against it.

Where was he?

He belonged here, with her, sharing this time, this
hour, this minute. Each and every minute away from him
was a minute lost, a minute they would never be able
to make up, no matter how hard they tried. She needed
him here with her; she needed his arms around her, his
strength, his maleness. And yet, he was not here and this
made no sense to her.

She turned from the door, shrugging out of the heavy
jacket she had been wearing, dropping it in a chair. She
went to the couch and lay down, seeking the warmth
she so desperately needed. Closing her eyes, she thought
back to the happiness of the early part of the afternoon,
the wonder and joy of just being with him, of sharing
his thoughts. It had been such a wonderful afternoon,

full of fun and laughter and friendship, the things that were important to her.

And then a wave of nausea swept over her and momentarily she fought against the rising suddenness of it and won her fight. She was remembering the scene on this very couch, the touch of his lips against hers, the sharp stabs of curiosity mingled with pain as his mouth had found her breasts. She had wanted to go farther; she had wanted to rip her clothing away, to bare herself before his eyes, to let him see the full beauty of her as a woman; and yet, at the same time, something unseen and unknown was holding her back, forcing her to say no and to continue saying no.

What was wrong with her? Was she really a cold woman? What made her go so far and then back away at the last moment? She loved him and sooner or later she was going to have him—this she knew. There was no reason for avoiding it. She had avoided it before with all the others, and now she was avoiding it with him. But there was no man like him and this should have changed the whole scope of things for her. There was a kind of tragic brittleness about him, as if he were afraid of letting anyone get too close to him, understanding him, helping him, loving him. She wanted to protect him from himself and immediately knew that this was wrong; he was too strong to need protection, yet there was something about him that seemed to cry out to the world in general and she wanted, above all else, to answer that cry.

The phone rang suddenly and she leaped up to answer it, hoping against hope that it would be Harry. It was her sister.

"Did you have a nice time this afternoon?" Margaret asked.

"Wonderful." She closed her eyes, gripping the receiver tightly.

"Did—did Harry come?"

"Yes. Jack and Maria came also. We went for a swim and had a picnic. Nothing too exciting."

"Are you all right, Grace?"

"Of course."

"Your voice sounds funny."

"I was lying on the couch, half-asleep." Why couldn't it have been Harry?

"Harry isn't there now, is he?"

"Margaret, are you checking up on me? I'm certainly mature enough to handle my own affairs."

"I'm not checking up on you! What's the matter with you, Grace? Can't I even call you and ask how you are?"

"I'm sorry." She was; Margaret meant well.

"You should be. Grace, you've changed recently. You simply aren't acting like yourself. Thomas has noticed it, too. What's wrong?"

"Nothing is wrong, Margaret."

"You don't want to tell me."

"Margaret, I have a headache and I'm tired. It's been a long day."

"Take two aspirins and go right to bed. You probably need a good night's sleep."

"I'll do that. G'night, Margaret."

She replaced the phone and stood there a moment, her shoulders slumped, a small dizziness whirring in her head. Two aspirins and go right to bed. Sure. That's great . . . go right to bed. A lonely bed; a huge bed with clean sheets and soft blankets and two fluffy pillows, and only one head to lie on those pillows, only one body to ·lie in the bed. What was wrong with her? She didn't need aspirin; she didn't need anything but a man, a certain man, strong and willing and gentle, a man who could guide her along the pathways to passion, stir up those dormant emotions within her, make her beg him to love her and crush her and take her . . .

She moved on unsure legs into the bedroom, stumbled against the side of the bed, almost falling. She stood in the half-light coming from the other room and slowly began to remove her clothing; she stripped down until she was nude and then walked into the bathroom, switching on the light there, staring at herself in the mirror. She was so very, very beautiful, she admitted to herself, sensing that it would be foolish for her to deny it; she had heard it so many times from so many different men and she knew that she epitomized a certain sexual connotation in the minds of most men. Beautiful Grace. Lovely Grace. Cold Grace.

She shuddered, backing away from the mirror, yet her eyes were fastened on her reflection. Her hands came up beneath the fullness of her breasts, lifted them gently and she saw the dark rosiness around her nipples. Harry had touched her there with his hands and with his mouth and she had felt the growing turmoil within her at his touch and then had forced that turmoil back, not wanting to let herself go. But why? Why not?

"My God," she said to herself, her voice strained and husky, "what's wrong with you, Grace? What is it with you?"

They all asked that same question eventually, all the men with whom she had been involved. Jack and Ramon and Jim, and now Harry. They wanted to know what was wrong with her, why she wouldn't let them do as they wished with her. She could not explain it; she had never been able to explain it, not even to herself. There was, in the back of her mind, a kind of contentment in knowing that she was going to be pure on her wedding night, that when her husband lifted her in his arms and carried her to their bed, she would be sweet, untouched, virginal. And then, at the right moment, she would change into a throbbing, passionate woman, the way they did in books, and everything would be just fine.

Yes. Everything would be just fine.

There would be some kind of magic key to change

her from what she was into what she wanted to be; there had to be a key because she knew that she couldn't continue as she was, confused and inwardly torn.

All these years . . .

She remembered when she had been seventeen and the boy's name was Lucius. He had been blond and not as tall as she, but still strong and muscular, full of laughter and sly jokes and he had been her date for the class picnic at the beach. They had wandered off by themselves, found a small nook in the sand hidden from the rest of the world, and they had lain down together side by side, and the warm sun had beat down on them, warming them. Before she had known that it was happening, he had slipped out of his trunks and was kneeling beside her, and she had looked at him, and her hand had gone to him and held him, and that was all that he had wanted. Afterward, she had felt dirty and slimy . . .

There had been the others after that, yet she had never allowed herself to touch them like that and she would never allow them to touch her.

She shook her head, said aloud, "Cut it out; cut out this torturing of yourself. You're a woman and you know it and the time will come when you can prove it."

She stepped into the tiled shower, turned on the cold water, drew in her breath as the shock of cold struck her skin . . .

Hennings closed the book he had been reading and looked up as his wife entered the bedroom. He saw her slight frown and he wondered what was bothering her now. Probably Grace. She had been worried about Grace recently, and he could understand that. Grace had been running around with Harry Mercer and he knew that Mercer was not the kind of a man who would stand meekly at the door and wait for a peck on the cheek.

No, he would take what he could when he could. Well, Grace was old enough to make her own decisions, Hennings told himself. Perhaps if Grace made a mistake or two, she would be better off in the long run.

"I like Sunday nights," he said.

"What?" Margaret was by her dresser, removing her earrings.

"I said I like Sunday nights."

"Yes, I know."

He watched her sit before the mirror, begin the nightly ritual of brushing her hair exactly one hundred times. He began counting silently to himself and then gave it up and looked around the room, which was warm and comfortable and he loved it. For Hennings, the room was a kind of milepost marking how far he had come in life, a symbol of the private life he shared with this woman —his woman—and the things they liked to do in the utmost privacy, without anyone else knowing about them. He doubted if many marriages were based on such firm foundations as was his and Margaret's; the years had been good to them, both of them, and now he was relaxed, looking ahead to the future. He had come a long way since meeting Margaret, and he had a long way still to go.

His eyes drifted back to her, saw that she had stopped her brushing and had turned to face him, sitting sort of slumped over. She was wearing a filmy pink negligee that he had given her on her last birthday and, beneath that, a rose-colored nightgown of nylon chiffon. He could see the mounds of her breasts beneath the nightgown and a vague stirring of desire reached at him, held for a moment. He knew that he was not the man he had been before, yet there had never been a moment when he doubted his ability to satisfy this woman.

"Thomas?"

"What?"

"Grace isn't—" she shook her head, not finishing. "I'm worried about her."

"I know you are, Margaret."

"I don't want to butt in where I'm not wanted."

"My God, Margaret, she's twenty-five years old. She's an intelligent adult with her own likes and dislikes, her own way of living. You can't live her life for her, no matter how much you would like to do so."

She raised the brush she was holding in her hand, looked at it for a moment, then placed it carefully on the dresser top. "I don't want to live her life for her," she said, "and you know better than that. I just don't want her to get hurt."

"Sometimes a little hurt helps us grow up."

She looked at him carefully. "Thomas, you're a very wise man, and I love you dearly. But I wish you wouldn't say things like that. Grace is getting in too deep with this Harry Mercer, and I can't see anything but anguish for her in the long run."

"You're always wanting her to get married."

"Of course. But you can take one look at Harry Mercer and know that he'll never get married."

"Are you sure?"

"What's your opinion, Thomas?"

He chuckled. "Mercer is like some wild bird, zooming over as much space as he can possibly cover. Perhaps when he's a good deal older and it takes him just a little longer to get over his drunks and his sexual forays, he might find himself a solid, respectable woman who isn't too interested in his past and settle down. But he won't marry Grace, of that I'm sure."

"Then doesn't it worry you that she—?"

"Margaret, Margaret," he interrupted soothingly. "Let her make her own mistakes. Let her run after him if she wants to. Let her find out what a man like Mercer is really like. She thinks of him as some romantic nomad of the present-day world. He isn't that at all. If we leave her alone, she'll find out soon enough."

"And in the meantime, she's going through the pangs of

loneliness and despair," she said. "I know her, Thomas. She won't give herself to him, and that's all he'll want."

"Maybe it's time she tried."

"Thomas!" Margaret looked at him, grinning slyly. "Sometimes you're impossible. Grace has been raised properly and prudently and she's not going to hop into bed with the first foot-loose reporter that happens to appeal to her."

"But you did," he said, smiling.

She rose, removing the negligee, dropping it on the foot of the bed. "Yes," she said. "And you remind me of that every chance you get. It just so happens that I felt sorry for you, that I didn't think any other woman could possibly be so stupid as to allow you to make love to her."

He laughed. "I love you, Margaret."

"I know you do, Thomas."

Those vague stirrings of desire took hold of him again, rousing him to a sudden pitch and he saw the look in her eyes as she glanced at him, the quick way she tossed her head to one side and ran her hands down the front of her nightgown.

"It's warm tonight," she said.

"Very."

He rose to his feet, removing his dressing gown. This was a small game they played together, a game each enjoyed, a game that had gone on for years and years.

"I don't think I'll need this tonight," she said, and slipped the nightgown quickly and efficiently over her head.

He knew every nook and cranny of her body, yet the sight of it like this never failed to stir him and, as he stepped out of his pajamas he saw the way her lips drew back tightly against her teeth as she viewed him.

"You're not worried about Grace now?" he asked teasingly.

"Oh, Thomas!" she said hurriedly.

He took a step toward her, then stopped. She lay on the bed, her hands outstretched to him.

"Come to me, Thomas," she whispered urgently. "Come to me and let me feel your passion and let me ride with you up and up, through the glories."

He laughed nervously, not wanting to rush it, wanting to simply stand beside the bed and gaze down at her and know that he could take her at any time he wished.

"Hurry, Thomas!"

He took her then, feeling her sharp intake of breath, and then they were both lost in the long luxury of their mutual rhythm . . .

five

HARRY felt the small, nagging doubt in the back of his mind as he sat in Henning's office, one leg crossed over the other. The hustle and bustle of the newspaper office was going on just behind him, yet he was oblivious to it this morning. He had awakened expecting to find Bess by his side, wanting her that one more time, and had found her gone. She had crept away in the night, and he had been strangely disappointed.

Now, as the office door opened and Thomas Hennings entered, he looked at the older man and wondered if he should tell him he was going to quit. He had been debating that all morning and still had not come to any definite conclusion.

"You wanted to see me, Mr. Hennings?"

Hennings was holding a sheaf of copy paper in his right hand, glancing at it. "Just a moment, please," he said, then tossed the sheaf of paper in his OUT box and sat down. He was, as always, meticulously dressed, looking as if he had had a full night's sleep and as if the whole world was going just right for him. In a way, Harry envied him.

"You're a pretty good writer, Mercer."

"I hope so. I think so. I've written enough stories by now to know how to put the words down in the right order."

"A lot of reporters never reach that point."

"That's their problem, Mr. Hennings."

"Of course." Hennings hesitated, made a temple with his fingers and peered through the temple at Harry. "Are you happy here, Mercer? You've had a little time to get acquainted, see our little city, meet the people you work with."

"Does it make any difference whether or not I'm happy?"

Something flickered in back of Hennings' eyes. He straightened up in his chair, ran a hand slowly along the contours of his face.

"Mercer," he said slowly, deliberately, "I like a man who is blunt, who gets to the point right away. But I also am appreciative of courtesy, and you seem to have forgotten all the rules by which we human beings exist. If you wish to be rude and uncouth, please do me the courttesy of behaving that way with others and not with me."

Harry felt the back of his neck burning. He had been properly chastised and he understood this; he also understood that he had deserved Hennings' words and now he searched his mind for some way to climb out of the hole in which he had gotten himself.

"I had a rough night, Mr. Hennings," he said. "I'm in a lousy mood this morning, feeling sorry for myself and maybe a little angry at the world. I'm apologizing."

"Good. I don't imagine it's something you often do."

"No, I don't have that habit."

"Are you happy here, Mercer?"

Harry hesitated, then shrugged. "Are you asking as my

employer or as the brother-in-law of Grace Wallace?"

Hennings leaned back in his chair, laughing slightly. "Perhaps a little of both."

"I suppose I'm as happy as I can be. This is a well-run paper you've got yourself here, though I haven't always agreed with the way you slant some of your stories."

"That's my right—to do as I wish. I told you that before you came to work here."

Harry grinned. "I guess you did, at that. It's your money and your paper."

Hennings also grinned. "I'm glad you see it that way," he said. "I've been thinking of running a series of articles on Beach City as a community. You know the kind of thing, its growth pattern and development, the kinds of people who are coming in and those who have been here all along. Maybe a little of the history going back to the land grant days, the days of the Spanish dons. I think you, as a newcomer to our city, might do a good job on this. You'd have to dig around, come up with a few different angles, but I'm sure you could do it. Sound interesting to you?"

"Sounds fine."

"Good. Starting this moment, it's your assignment. I'll let the city desk know, so they won't expect anything else from you. I'll want to see a rough outline of what you're planning in a day or two. Okay?"

"I'm happy, Mr. Hennings," Harry said. "You don't have to push it."

"You're a difficult man to get along with, Mercer. I'd hate to be the woman who eventually puts a rope around your neck and brings you in."

Harry rose. "I don't think that'll ever happen, Mr. Hennings. In fact, I'd be willing to bet on it."

Hennings only laughed, turning away from him.

Harry sat alone in the back booth of the coffeeshop,

smoking his third successive cigarette. He had called Jack Perkins from the office, asking the young banker to meet him here. He thought Perkins would be a good starting point for the articles he was going to write; the man was a native of Beach City and was bucking the tide of thought in his social circle; he was also intelligent and searching, and should be able to give Harry some definite opinions about Beach City.

His thoughts idled back over his talk with Hennings. Something about the talk bothered him; it was more what had not been said than what had been. All through the talk he had expected Hennings to make some mention of Grace. The newspaper owner definitely was not a man to sit back and watch a woman close to him make a fool of herself by chasing after a man who did not want her.

But the point was that he, Harry, did want Grace; the only difference was that he did not want her in the same way that she wanted him, and he wondered if Hennings realized this. In a way, he was sorry that he had ever come to Beach City and had allowed himself to become entangled with these people. For, no matter how hard he tried to convince himself otherwise, he realized that he was entangled with them, and that was something he wished mightily that he could have avoided.

"A lonely man with his lonely thoughts," Jack Perkins said, approaching the booth.

"Nuts," Harry snapped, and then laughed.

Perkins, too, laughed, sliding into the booth opposite Harry. "That's what I like about you, Harry," he said. "You get right to the point, no mishmashing around before hand."

"How's the banking business today?"

"Full of money." Perkins ran a hand over his receding hairline, pursing his lips. "You look tired out, my friend."

"I am tired out," he said, "but not from what you

think. Or maybe it is from what you think, but not with whom you think."

"Well, better luck next time. They say that after dark all cats are gray, anyway. Do you think it's true?"

"Hell, no!" Harry said.

"I didn't think so."

The waitress came and they both ordered lunch.

"Hennings has given me a good assignment," Harry said. "He wants me to write a series of articles on your fair city. I thought maybe a good place to start would be with you."

"And I thought you just wanted my company for lunch."

"That, too, buddy-boy."

"What do you want from me?"

"Anything, everything. Just tell me what you think of Beach City, maybe how it was growing up here, how it's changed, how it looks through your eyes."

"Will I be quoted?"

"Not if you don't want to be."

"I don't. I'm chicken that way."

"We're all chicken, one way or the other."

"Well, let's see," Perkins said, leaning forward, resting his elbows on the table. "It was great here when I was a kid. I thought the sun rose and set right here in Beach City. There were the wonderful beaches, uncrowded; the smooth white sand uncluttered with beer cans and Kleenex and trash, and a guy could go and be by himself if he wanted to or sneak off with a girl and not have hundreds of others peering at you like you were some kind of a nut. Is this the kind of thing you want?"

"Exactly right."

"You're not taking notes."

"I won't need them. I'm just getting impressions."

Perkins went on; he talked right through lunch and for fifteen or twenty minutes afterward, and Harry, listening to him, got the idea that the man was getting something

off his chest, ridding himself of something that had been
bothering him for a long while . . .

That was Harry's first interview. He spent the rest of
the afternoon walking around the downtown section, talking to people. He talked to a small, gnarled little man
with cruel eyes who owned a cigar store, with a bird-
faced woman who ran a beauty parlor, a sad-eyed cab
driver, the publicity man for the chamber of commerce,
the principal of a high school, the owner of a cleaning
establishment.

When he was finished, he realized that he was tired
and worn out from listening to everyone vent his or her
gripe against the inequities that could be found in any
city. He had a picture in his mind of this city, but whether
or not it was a true picture he could not be sure.

There seemed to be four definite class-lines in Beach
City. The real upper crust were the descendants of the
old Spanish land-grant families, clinging to the remnants
of their gloried past, having money and prestige, estate-
sized homes in the most fashionable part of the city, everything but actual social acceptance outside themselves.
The second class-line involved the families that actually
controlled the city. They were wealthy and hard-nosed,
biased against anyone outside their own little group, upset because the city was changing with the times. Hennings was one of the three or four most important men in
this group, and he seemed to have his fingers in everything. Through the power of owning the city's only newspaper, he had the habit of molding thoughts to his own
way of thinking. He was in a position, Harry surmised,
of being potentially a dangerous man—a man who could
have things almost his own way if he so desired.

The third class was the great middle, containing the
store-owners, the white-collar workers and the profession-
als who staffed the aircraft and electronics plants. Perhaps
half of these were almost as new to Beach City as Harry
himself, bringing with them a confusion of cultures and

backgrounds. Finally, there was the last class, composed
of the laborers and Mexicans, jumbled into a small area
near the railroad tracks, uneducated for the most part,
distrustful of authority, forced into their tiny, squalid
holes by the bigotry of the city around them. This was not
a racial bigotry as such, though there were many who
referred to the Mexicans in that area as "wetbacks;" rather it was a bigotry against the people themselves, regardless of their ethnic backgrounds.

Harry didn't like some of the thoughts that were going through his mind. He was too mature and had seen
too much of the world to consider himself a knight in
shining armor, ready and willing to battle all foes; yet he
was sincerely disturbed by some of the things he had discovered—the many forms of prejudice and bigotry; the
power of Hennings and his crowd; the general apathy of
most of the people—and he told himself that he would
present these things in his article, along with the history
of the place. That is, if Hennings would permit it.

When he got back to his hotel room, he was surprised
to find Bess sitting in one of the chairs, reading a book.

"Hi, sport," she said happily.

He stood there a moment, staring at her. She looked
particularly luscious this night and, as she rose and stared
back at him he saw the slight flicker of amusement in
her unusual eyes. She was wearing a gray silk dress with
a full skirt, pinched in at the waist to reveal the full
bloom of her breasts and a single strand of pearls dipped
into the deep V of the dress.

"You have a habit of being in the right place at the
right time," he said.

"You mean you're glad to see me?"

"I mean I'm glad to see you."

"I couldn't tell. You've got the most awful expression
on your face."

They stood there a moment silently, each conscious of the strong pull from the other, like two animals waiting for the right signal. Then, he passed a hand across his eyes and shook his head.

"How about my taking you to dinner?" he asked.

"Harry," she said, and then shrugged. "I don't know what to say to you, and that's a damned rare thing, believe me. I just wanted to see you, that's all. I was hoping you'd ask me, but I—oh, hell, do I have to explain it?"

"You don't have to explain anything, sweetheart. Just let me take a shower and change."

"Could I help?"

He felt genuine lust spreading through him; it seemed almost tangible, the way it grabbed him and held him, and he was only dimly aware of the fact that he had not felt this way about any one woman in a long time, perhaps too long. He wanted her because she was Bess, not because she was just any woman. And, fleetingly, that worried him.

He slowly began undressing. "I can see what happened to those husbands of yours. You probably killed them with love."

"Not love, Harry," she said, unsnapping her dress. "A little sex now and again, but not love."

It was weird, he thought, the way they could stand there so far apart from each other, stripping down, yet continuing to talk. He watched her step out of the dress, felt the full, strident force of his manhood leap to the fore as he looked at the beauty of her body. She was wearing only a brassiere, panty-girdle, and her nylons.

"Like?" she asked in a husky voice.

"Damn you!" he snapped.

"Come to me, baby," she said, stripping away the rest of her clothing and throwing herself on the bed. "Come to me. Oh, God, Harry, hurry!"

He was beside her and then over her, feeling her hand guiding him, feeling the luxury of her full lips enveloping his tongue, heard the sudden, sharp gasp of her breath.

It was long and slow, practiced, as if they had been making love to each other since the beginning of time; once, twice, three times he reached the peak, and each time, miraculously, he managed to wait for her, and then her nails were gouging into his back and her mouth was punishing his and the rapid sound of their breathing was lost in the moans of their mutual ecstasies . . .

He lay on his back, exhausted, staring at the ceiling above him. Her fingers touched him and she laughed.

"What's so funny?" he asked.

"You, you damned man, you," she replied. "One minute you're yelling to the world what a big, tough boy you are, and the next minute you're quiet and trying to hide away from everybody."

"You take a lot from a man," he said.

"Not just any man, Harry."

He turned his head, looking at her. She was lying on her back, her large, perfectly formed breasts rising and falling with her breathing. He placed his hand on the flatness of her stomach, rubbing gently. She turned, staring into his eyes.

"I was a girl once, Harry," she said, "a shy little girl who would blush if anyone even looked at me. I had these big breasts even then, and I tried to hide them so the boys wouldn't look at me and make fun of me.

"And then there was one boy, a special boy, and one more after that, and then I thought the whole world began and ended with having someone climb up on me and let me ride the high thrills with him. I was dumb, Harry, and I was gullible and I believed anything anyone told me."

"Why are you telling me this?"

"I'm not sure. I know what kind of a guy you are, Harry, and I know the long run isn't for you. You'll take what you can from me or any woman, and then you'll run over that hill to see what's on the other side. That's your kind and I don't blame you for it. If I were a man, I'd probably do the same thing and for the same reasons. I know I can't hold you, no matter how hard I might try, so I'm not even going to try. But I do want you to know me, Harry, know me as I really am, and not just a good girl in the hay who you might remember a year from now because I knew how to move my hips.

"I've got a reputation, sure. I've been married and divorced twice and, in this burg, that's enough to give anyone a reputation. But I'm not that easy and I never have been, even though I like it, and you know how much I like it."

She grinned and, for a brief moment, he could imagine her as a frightened, bewildered little girl with a woman's body, searching for a moment's peace of mind, searching for that solution that would forever elude her.

He moved his hand up, caressing one of her breasts, gently fingering the rosette nipple. He felt it grow rigid under his manipulation and he bent his head down, closing his lips on it, drawing it within his mouth, and once more her body began to move rhythmically . . .

six

JOHN ROSS sat for a moment longer in the car, his hands resting lightly on the steering wheel, wondering whether or not he should go into the house. He did not want to; he wanted to back the car out and head down the coast to Los Angeles and find his comfort there. He knew he would not find comfort within his own home.

Finally, he moved out of the car, standing in the semi-darkness of the garage interior a moment before walking outside. Daylight still clung tenaciously to the sky above him as he looked out over the expanse of rolling green lawn, neatly trimmed hedges and carefully nurtured strips of flower beds. He had been born in this house, had known it for all of his years, and still he always felt something like an intruder when he came home, as if it did not really belong to him and never could belong to him.

He remembered the time he was twelve and he had chased Monica Hendrix across that same lawn, trying to raise her skirt up so that he could see what was underneath and his mother had come rushing from the house like a wild, angry animal. Descending upon him, she had slapped him across the face, right in front of Monica, and had told him what a nasty, filthy little boy he was. His mother had taken him into the house and had wrapped his hands tightly in gauze so that he could not even move his fingers and she had made him go to bed that way. He had lain awake for a long time that night, trying to move his fingers within their tight bandages, picking at the gauze with his teeth, and he had heard his mother and his father arguing long into the night, viciously and harshly, using words that he knew were wrong . . .

A long time ago.

He was still, he thought, something like that little boy, only now he knew what would be underneath the skirt, and yet, with his wife, that did him no good at all. Damn her, damn her to hell! She was evil and domineering, just as his mother had been, and it seemed to him now that he had merely switched from one dominating woman to another; and suddenly he felt very sad, felt that his life was slipping away from him.

He shrugged and walked slowly, his shoulders slumped, across the fieldstone walk to the side of the house and entered through the kitchen. Veline, their Negro maid, was just coming into the kitchen from the other direction. She gave him a broad, happy smile. She had been a part of this house for almost as long as he could remember.

"My goodness, Mr. Ross," she said, "I wasn't expecting you home at this time."

He paused. "Why not, Veline?"

"The missus said you wouldn't be home for dinner, that's why not."

He frowned, searching through his mind. He had certainly not said anything to Cynthia about not being home for dinner.

"You feeling okay, Mr. Ross?"

"What?" He looked at Veline; she was short and muscular and, to him, ageless. "Oh, yes, I'm fine, Veline."

"You don't look so hot, Mr. Ross, you don't mind my saying so."

"Now, don't start mothering me again, Veline. I'm fine."

Veline raised a hand, touching him gently on the shoulder, then dropped the hand to her side. "I worry about you, Mr. Ross. Maybe you don't want me to, but I do just the same. I know what I see, and I been seeing a long time that you ain't too happy. You can't fool me, Mr. Ross, and there's no sense in your trying."

"That's enough, Veline."

"If you say so, Mr. Ross," she said defiantly, looking him right in the eye.

He walked around her, knowing that she had seen right through him; she was the one person he had never been able to fool. He had always been able to lie to his mother and get away with it, and his father had never paid any attention to him, anyway.

He walked through the silent house and up the stairs. As he opened the bedroom door, he heard the sound of the shower. He slipped out of his suit coat, loosened his tie, and slumped down on one of the twin beds.

Veline came in almost immediately after him, carrying a tray on which were glasses and a martini pitcher.

"This here'll fix you up fine, Mr. Ross," she said, placing the tray on the bedside table.

"You're a fine woman, Veline," he said.

"Oh, pshaw!" she exclaimed. "Don't give me none of your sweet talk now. You just pour yourself a coupla good ones and relax a bit. You want anything to eat, just let me know."

He sat up, stirred the mixture a bit, and poured himself a martini. Just as Veline closed the door behind her, the bathroom door opened and Cynthia, wrapped in a fluffy pink towel, padded into the room.

"Damn that Veline," Cynthia said. "She was in here snooping around again, wasn't she?"

"She was looking after me, if that's what you mean."

Cynthia laughed, pulling the towel closer around her, her hands gripped tightly together. "That's a hot one," she said. "You're a grown man, aren't you? Why in hell should anyone look after you? Jesus, you know what I think? I think that old bitch comes in here just hoping to catch us in bed together. I bet she gets her kicks that way."

"You've got a filthy mind, Cynthia!"

"Haven't I, though?"

"Sometimes I hate the sight of you."

"You don't know how to hate. You've been sucking hind-tit for your whole damned life and you'll continue doing it until you die."

"I ought to throw your ass right out of this house!"

"Go ahead. I dare you. You haven't got the nerve."

He sat there, looking at her, knowing that she was speaking the truth, knowing that he would never have the nerve; he never had had the nerve to do anything but what he was told. Her eyes danced mockingly as she stared back at him, and he wanted to rise up and slap her across the mouth, see the blood run from her lips, see those eyes change, see some semblance of respect come into them. She had mocked him for so long.

He was reaching the point where he was not sure if he could stand it much longer.

"You're pure bitch, Cynthia," he said.

"You're damned right I am," she replied. "I've never denied that, have I? Can I help it if you can't see what's as plain as the nose on your face?"

"Don't rub it in."

"Why don't you beg, John?"

He took a sip of his martini, then drained the whole glass.

She had moved away from him and was now brushing her hair before her mirror. Her hair fairly sparkled as she ran the brush through it, and he could remember the many times in the beginning when he had gripped that hair, holding on as if for dear life. Had she fooled him that much? Had he been that big a fool?

"Cynthia?"

"What now?" She did not bother to look at him.

"What's in this marriage for you?"

She paused, turning to look at him. "Money, prestige. I don't need anything else."

"What about me?"

"Well, what about you?"

"God, don't you have any compunctions, any morals?"

"Why should I, John? I was born to nothing in this damned world and everything I've got I've had to fight for. You don't think I ever enjoyed anything with you, do you? What kind of idiot are you, John? My God, sometimes I think you're about ten years old."

How could he have reached this point? All these years of breathing and living, dreaming and hoping, and now this. He was a man, and yet he was not a man; perhaps he was merely the figment of his own imagination, going through the motions of that other world, the real world.

He watched her as she deliberately stripped the towel away from her body, stood a moment before the mirror gazing at herself. He wondered if she really loved herself that much or if it was only pretense, a calculated theatrical bit to add to his misery. He was acutely conscious of her slim legs, narrow hips, the high, firm breasts, the dark, triangular apex of his desires as she swung around and walked boldly past him to the closet. He saw the smooth rippling of her buttocks as she rose on tiptoe to get something from the shelf, was aware of the faint smirk on her mouth as she passed him again, laying her clothes out on the other bed.

"You're going out," he said.

"That's a damned brilliant deduction."

The sudden flood of lust struck him in his middle, spread throughout his whole body, engulfing him in its intensity. He was almost shamed by it, knowing what kind of woman stood naked before him, what kind of woman he had married. Although she was not a woman in the real sense, he could not deny the power she held over him. If he could only possess her one more time, perhaps then he would be able to rid himself of her, to drive the memories of his passion for her from his mind.

He forced the desires back, knowing they would come to nothing, and reached across, refilling his glass, gulping half of the martini immediately.

"Why did you tell Veline I wouldn't be home for dinner?"

"I don't know. I wasn't sure you would be. Who cares?"

"I care, Cynthia. I care very much."

"That's too bad."

"Where are you going?"

She straightened up, turning to face him, her hands at her sides, a woman whom, by all rights and laws, he should have been able to possess, yet could not.

"If you must know," she said, "I'm having dinner with Grace."

"What am I supposed to do?"

She shrugged. "Sit here and get drunk for all I care. Maybe if you get drunk enough—" she grinned "—when

I get home, we can see what happens."

"You mean if you don't find anyone else to satisfy your perverted desires?"

"That's a nice way of putting it, John." She placed a hand on the dark triangle, rubbing slowly. "Look, it wouldn't be so bad, really. Just try it once, that's all I ask. Hell, John, it's only sex, nothing more."

He sat there and felt the blood pumping through him; he heard the beat of his heart thumping against his chest, and again he saw the mockery in her eyes, the disdain in which she held him, ridiculing him for what he was. For a brief moment, clear and sharp, he saw the failure that he was, that he had always been, that he always would be. Then, without being conscious of it, a deep growling sound came from his throat, and he leaped toward her.

His sudden attack caught her by surprise. The weight of his body knocked her back across the bed and she lay there for a moment in numbed shock, watching him rip away his clothes. Then realization came to her, and she tried to jump from the bed at the other side. His quickness was amazing; one strong hand gripped her shoulder, twisting her around, pulling her back. His other hand slapped her across the face and a thin trickle of blood oozed from the corner of her mouth.

"You're my wife!" he screamed. "I have my rights!"

"Goddamn you!" she screamed back at him.

She writhed beneath him, trying to fight her way free; but he was far too strong for her. His arms pinioned her shoulders to the bed and his mouth descended against hers, tasting the salty blood. She tried to bite back at him, and he moved his head just in time. He forced her legs apart, laughing, enjoying this now, knowing that he was winning, knowing that, finally, he was showing her —and himself—what kind of man he was. He heard the sharp intake of her breath as he entered, and suddenly she was relaxing beneath him. He raised his head to look down at her face. She was grinning up at him, that mockery still dancing in her eyes.

"Go ahead, John," she said. "Enjoy yourself. Because it doesn't mean a single damned thing to me."

Then he wanted to cry out; he wanted to stop, and yet he could not. He could only continue and try not to think of the way she was looking at him, try not to think that she was completely unresponsive beneath him, taunting him more than she had ever done before . . .

He lay in a heap on one side of the bed, breathing deeply, realizing that he had raped his own wife and that, in the act of raping her, he had lost himself forever. No matter how long he lived, he could never erase from his mind the image of her looking up and laughing at him. The knowledge that he had not even touched her with his passion, that she had been miles from him, hurt worse than anything else he could imagine. He heard her walking in the room, yet he kept his eyes closed, not wanting to look at her, afraid of what he would see.

"I hope you had a good time, John." Her voice reached him as if from a far distance. "I didn't think you were man enough to do that," she said.

Still he lay there, unmoving, unspeaking.

"It's a pity, John," she went on. "It really is. You've been saving yourself for so long, and it really wasn't worth it, was it? You got yourself all upset for nothing."

"Go away," he mumbled.

"I'm going. Maybe tonight I'll find someone who can really satisfy me, someone who knows all the little tricks that you don't. You know what you are, John? You're a mama's boy, a poor, weak, little mama's boy, and any real woman would laugh at the best attempts you could ever make. You're dumb, John, just too dumb, ever to learn what makes things work."

He tried to shut the sound of her voice from his mind. He did not want to listen to her; he wanted to be safe and secure within the walls of himself, safe from people like her, safe from that cruel world that bred people like her and forced them to enter into his world . . .

He heard the front door open and close, and then there was only the silence of his own being. He opened his eyes and sat up in the middle of the bed.

Why? he asked himself. Why had this happened?

He shuddered and lay back, cradling his head in his arms, wanting to cry, wanting the hot, cleansing tears to flow through his closed eyelids . . .

Grace sat quietly at the table in the corner, listening to the sounds of the restaurant around her. She liked this place, Pico's, and usually she would be enjoying herself, but a dark cloud hung over her tonight and she wondered why. She glanced again at her watch, wondering what was keeping Cynthia; she was almost an hour late.

"Everything fine, Miss Wallace?"

She glanced up at Pico's warm, friendly face.

"Everything's fine, Pico."

"That is good," the chubby little Mexican said. "You are special here with us, Miss Wallace."

"My friend is late, that's all."

"Ah, the world goes at too fast a speed."

"Perhaps you're right, Pico."

He moved away and she glanced at the tables around her. Pico's was a warm, delightful place, specializing in the best steaks in Beach City. The tables were covered with red-and-white checked tablecloths and a small candle, stuck in the top of an empty wine bottle, burned brightly in the center of each table.

She glanced at her watch again, and frowned. It was unlike Cynthia to be this late and a breath of concern touched her, then vanished as she saw her friend walking toward her.

"I'm so very sorry to be so late," Cynthia said, gripping Grace's extended hand tightly. "That damned husband of mine was simply impossible tonight."

Grace smiled. "I'm glad you could come, at any rate."

"God!" Cynthia exclaimed, sitting down and sighing deeply, "I could stand a drink. You'd never believe what happened to me tonight." She grinned mysteriously. "Come on, Grace, have another one with me. I just can't bring myself to face any food yet."

"Well—all right."

"Don't be so prudish, Grace. If you have more than one drink no one is going to know, and it certainly isn't going to hurt you any."

Grace laughed. Cynthia was right, as she always had been. There was no harm in having another drink; certainly nothing could happen to her tonight. But, even after she had signaled the waiter and he had brought another manhattan for Grace and a double martini for Cynthia, Grace felt a trifle guilty; she was not accustomed to drinking and she did not want to get into the habit.

"We haven't been seeing much of each other," Grace said. "Not like it was in the old days."

"Don't you worry, honey," Cynthia said, reaching across, caressing Grace's hand lightly. "We're still friends and we always will be."

"I do hope so," Grace said, and immediately blushed at the feeling in her tone; she had not meant it that way. She had never been able to understand Cynthia fully, the way she could change so quickly had always puzzled Grace. She was something like a chameleon in that respect, changing her coloring to fit the situation. When Cynthia had married John Ross, Grace had been surprised; she had always imagined that Cynthia would be one of those who would shake Beach City from her background, go to some big city like New York or San Francisco or Los Angeles and devote her life to being a successful business woman.

"Come on, Grace. Cheer up! Don't sit there and look at me with that long, sad face like that. The world isn't going to end this very minute."

"I didn't think it was."

"Honestly, you don't realize how lucky you are. I wish to hell that I were single again, able to play the field the way you are. You can't imagine what it's like being tied down to the same man all the time."

"I guess I can't. Anyway, Cynthia, you know very well that I don't play the field."

"Well, just listen to some sage advice from an old friend and never get yourself all tangled up with one man." Cynthia glanced around her, then shook her head from side to side. "You simply wouldn't believe what happened to me tonight."

"You said that before," she said, and immediately wished that she had not. She did not want to hear about Cynthia's personal life. She knew that her friend was having trouble with John, and she did not wish to sit here and listen to the woes of that marriage. She had enough problems of her own, and she wondered why she had even bothered asking Cynthia to have dinner with her tonight.

Cynthia had lit a cigarette and was now puffing it quickly. She seemed nervous, keyed up, as if she were expecting something unpleasant to happen to her at any moment.

"Grace," she said, looking around furtively, "that bastard John actually raped me tonight! Can you imagine that?"

"Really, Cynthia, I don't think—"

"Can you believe that a man would do that—to his own wife? I couldn't believe that he was serious. That's why I was so late. I was getting ready to meet you and he came home and simply threw me down on the bed, as if I were some common whore that he could do with as he pleased. I don't know what got in to him." She puffed on the cigarette again, exhaling great volumes of smoke. "I feel—I don't know, degraded I guess. I've never been raped before."

Grace closed her eyes and looked away. What a thing to be telling someone! She tried not to visualize the scene, but the pictures kept developing within her mind against her will, and she saw the nude form of Cynthia beneath John, both grunting and sweating like animals and Cynthia kept beating him on the back, yelling for him to stop this nonsense, and he kept ignoring her—

"I guess I've shocked you," Cynthia said. "I didn't mean to."

"I don't shock that easily." She smiled gravely. "I really don't think you should have told me, though."

"For heaven's sake, why not?"

She hesitated. What could she say? She could only wish that there were a hole some place where she could go and hide her head and forget all these problems, forget what Cynthia had just told her, forget the depths of her feelings for Harry, forget what she knew about Maria and Jack, forget everything. She had come here seeking relief from her own worries and instead had only added to them. Nothing seemed to be going right for her.

"I guess I opened my big mouth once too often," Cynthia said, "but I had to tell someone."

"I know."

"Do you?"

"Well—maybe not really. But I can imagine."

"How are you and that Harry character doing?"

"He isn't a character."

Cynthia laughed. "That tells me enough. I thought I saw enough the night of the party. Now I know. You're stuck on him."

The waiter brought their menus. The letters seemed to swim before Grace's eyes.

"You'll get over it, honey," Cynthia said. "He's nothing. There's no reason why—"

"Is there ever a reason?"

"Don't be a romantic fool, Grace. My God, you're old enough by now to know the score. You simply can't get involved with a man because you think of him as some romantic adventurer who has managed to avoid working in this country for several years."

"I'd rather not discuss it, Cynthia." She had the feeling that this woman across from her was a stranger, not someone with whom she had shared so many secrets for years past.

"Is it that bad?"

"Just let it alone, Cynthia. Please."

"Okay, so I'm trying to stick my nose in where it's not wanted. But listen to me for once, Grace. I've played the old game and I know what I'm talking about. He wants nothing more from you than your body. All men are alike. My God, I learned that a long time ago. Give them an inch and they'll take you for everything you've got."

"Please, Cynthia."

"Does the truth hurt?"

She finished her drink and nodded at the waiter.

"Don't let him do it, Grace," Cynthia said.

There was something strange in Cynthia's attitude, something that Grace had never sensed before. It was almost as if this was a new Cynthia, a Cynthia who had become hardened and embittered.

"Whatever I do will be of my own choosing," Grace said.

"Perhaps," Cynthia said after the waiter had left with their orders, "and perhaps not. You know how I was about John in the beginning. I don't think it's any secret to you that he and I were sharing the same bed before we got married. I let him do that to me, but I lost something when I did."

Cynthia's hand was smoothly caressing hers, almost with desire, and she looked across at the married woman and felt a shocking moment of fright before Cynthia pulled her hand back.

She was in a daze for the rest of the evening, unable to comprehend what was going on around her, knowing only that something valuable had gone out of her life. She had always admired Cynthia, and now the other woman made her uncomfortable, sent thoughts through her head that she did not want to think. Could it be that Cynthia was not the person she had always admired? Could it be that she was wrong about so many things?

They were halfway through dinner when Grace looked up and saw Harry and Bess Higgins following Pico to a table near them. Grace almost choked on her food. She felt a deep flush spreading throughout her whole body and her throat suddenly became dry. She quickly gulped down some water and tried to look the other way, tried to ignore the fact that he was sitting there, so close to her, yet with another woman, a woman like Bess Higgins.

"You don't need to pretend," Cynthia said. "I saw them, too."

Grace felt so small, so vulnerable. Why?

"I don't know what he sees in that woman," Cynthia was saying. "Everyone knows she's the easiest thing in town for any man who wants her."

Grace tried hard not to look. She could see the sharp outline of Harry's profile, the way he was turning his head, the quick recognition in his eyes and the slow grin spreading over his lips. He looked somehow tired and drawn, his shoulders slightly slumped. She felt she had to do something so she nodded in his direction and he nodded in return and that was all.

She felt the tightness start in her stomach. She had never before been jealous, but at that moment she would have willingly crossed to that other table and torn every hair from Bess Higgins's head. She hated her; she loathed her. It should have been she, Grace, sitting there with him, laughing easily with him, knowing the strength that was within him and the love she held for him.

"I'm going," she whispered to Cynthia.

"You can't run out. He isn't worth that."

"I'm going," she repeated.

Harry toyed with the glass in his hand, watching Grace walk stiff-legged, her shoulders back, her lips set in a straight line; she looked straight ahead and marched right out of the place. In a way, he felt almost sorry for her.

"If looks could kill," Bess said slowly, "I'd be stone-cold dead right now."

"Don't be silly."

"I'm not. She hates my guts."

He tried to laugh. "She has no reason to."

"Don't give me that, lover," she said. "I saw the glint in your eyes when you saw her. I told you a long time ago, I don't blame you. She's quite a gal. And I also told you what you'd have to do to get her."

He looked across at Bess. The shine of happiness in her eyes was dimmed slightly. He wished that he could understand her; he wished that he could understand any woman.

"I'm happy," he said.

"Are you?" There was the barest hint of self-castigation in her tone. "Maybe, maybe not. Sure, you've just had a good time with me and you're remembering that, how good it was between us. But I'm wondering what you would have done if she had raised her finger to you, told you to come on with her and you could do what you want."

"Cut it out, Bess."

"Shouldn't I be jealous?"

"That's stupid and you know it."

"I know nothing," she said. "I'm only available and around when you want me, that's all." The tears welled up behind her eyes and she quickly shook her head, not looking at him. "I'm sorry, Harry. I'm acting like any other damned fool woman right now, and I don't want to act that way. I told you before, no strings attached. We both know what we want, and we both know how to get it."

"That's for sure," he said.

She looked at him for a long, slow moment, and then said, "I wish I didn't have my past."

"Don't worry about what you've done before, Bess," he said. "It isn't worth the bother. You can't take it back; it's done and finished, and no matter how hard you try you'll never be able to change it."

"Right now—right at this moment—I wish I could."

"Why?"

"Don't ask that, Harry."

"I am asking it."

"All right, you want to know. Maybe if I were sweet and virginal and didn't have two ex-husbands you'd look at me the way you look at Grace. Sure, I'm jealous. I don't deny it."

"You're going feminine on me."

"Why shouldn't I?"

"I don't know."

"God, Harry," she said. "You've got a rock for a heart."

"I'm only being myself."

"I don't think you are."

"Don't try to psychoanalyze me, Bess. I've had that done to me too many times, especially by amateurs."

"Nuts," she said, and turned her face away.

"You're sounding like me now."

She closed her eyes, opened them again. "We're arguing now, something we haven't done before."

"It always ends this way."

"Who said anything about ending it?"

He shrugged. He was thinking of so many things; he was thinking that Grace had gotten to him, right into the pit of his stomach, and he was thinking that he was not being fair to treat Bess this way. It had been a long time since he had thought about being fair to a woman, and now he glanced at the soft sheen of her hair, remembered the deep passions they had shared, and wondered if that was all any man and woman ever shared. But there just had to be more than that.

"Be nice to me, Bess," he said. "I'm a lonely man and I need someone to be nice to me."

"You mean—?"

"I mean just be yourself. I like you when you're that."

She gave him a tentative smile, and he was grateful for that small bit of solicitude. He knew that he did not deserve it; he was taking from her and giving her nothing in return and that was not right, no matter how he tried to rationalize it. He was suddenly ashamed of himself, of what he was, of how he was treating this woman.

"It's a bitch of a life, isn't it?" he asked.

A couple at the next table was laughing merrily and happily. She looked at them for a moment before answering, then said, "I guess it's what we make of it, Harry."

"I guess it is," he said, and thought of all the things he had made of his life. Most of all, he thought of how alone he was.

seven

GRACE awakened to the cooling ocean breeze coming through her opened bedroom window. She gulped in the fresh air, wishing that she did not have to stir from the bed. She rolled on to her side, feeling the gnawing pit of loneliness within her. She was far too old to awake each morning like this, alone and unloved, and blindly her hand strayed along the other side of the bed, searching for the body that she knew would not be there. It had never been there and she was beginning to wonder if it would ever be there; she was beginning to doubt herself.

She heard the faint call of a boy's voice from along the beach, and then a dog's joyous barking broke through. She imagined a boy walking along the beach, his dog at his heels, laughing and bursting at the seams with life, ready and willing to face anything that might come along. She wondered if Harry had ever been like that or if, by some peculiar magic, he had managed to skip that part of his childhood. She wished that she knew more about him, all the little things that a woman should know about the man she loves.

She breathed deeply, then rolled from beneath the blankets, and sat on the edge of the bed. She knew that she could not continue like this; something had to break, sooner or later. She could not continue to possess Harry in her thoughts and yet reject him in the reality of his own world; and above all, she knew she could not blame him for mistrusting her if she did that.

She rose and slipped out of the brief nightie, standing nude and slightly cold before the opened window. Was he, too, just awakening, standing beside his bed? She tried to picture him there, his muscular nude body bared before her gaze, and a warm flush spread throughout her, bringing a quickening to her pulse. If he were here now, this very moment, she would let him do with her as he wished, and she would not back away. She wondered if she would scream in pain; she had read so many things and had heard so many things, and the thought of actually going through with it, of lying back on the bed with Harry crouching before her, smiling at her in that special way of his, and then hurting her, frightened her a great deal. She swung away from the window, turned her back to it. She did not want to feel this way; millions of women, she knew, went through this act, and she was no different from any of them. There was nothing special about her; she had nothing that any of the others didn't have.

She shuddered, walking into the living room, knowing that she could not face a room full of children this day. She called the school and told the secretary that she was not feeling well and would not be in.

She called Maria Nevarez and made a luncheon date with her. She walked back into the bedroom and suddenly her whole being seemed to scream out with a want of Harry. For a fleeting moment, she visualized him, coming into the bedroom, sweeping her up in his arms, and then everything was whirling before her eyes.

Maria looked beautiful, fresh and virginal, almost as if she were a vision and could not possibly be real. She was standing at one side of the small, darkened alcove of the tea room, wearing a flowered print dress and a large hat. She extended a hand in Grace's direction as the latter approached.

There was the subdued tinkle of silverware and the rich hushed sound of women's voices as Maria and Grace were led to a table at the wide windows overlooking the ocean. Grace sighed contentedly as she sat down and began removing her gloves; this was her world, the world with which she was so familiar, the world in which she had been bred and raised. How many times had she and her sister and their friends had lunch in this tea room? It was a place where men were virtually forbidden; the sight of a man usually caused all conversation to cease until he was properly sized up and classified.

"A day off from the howling youngsters?" Maria asked.

"Honestly, Maria," she said, "I just don't think I could've taken them today. I needed a morning by myself, a luncheon with someone like you."

"That's a nice compliment."

"I mean it."

Grace looked out the window now, at the strange calmness of the waves below them; there were hardly any whitecaps visible. A distant motorboat skimmed past, towing a water-skier in its wake. She would not be able to take many more mornings like this one, absently moving from one room of her house to the other, picking up things, putting them down again, going for a brief swim. She had tried so hard to convince herself that she was doing the wrong thing in chasing after Harry, yet she had failed to do so. She knew only that she wanted him, and that she was determined to have him.

"You're pensive now," Maria said, after they had ordered.

"Perhaps."

"A woman alone is a woman in need."

"What does that mean?"

"You know what it means, Grace."

"I guess I do. I suppose I just wanted you to explain it to me. Oh, Maria—" she reached across, clenching Maria's hand tightly in her own—"I just don't know! I'm running around in circles, searching for what is right and what is wrong."

"The answer would depend on you."

"Yes."

"You are so alone, Grace. You've always been alone, as long as I've known you. I don't hold that against you, I'm sure you understand that. But you withhold yourself, Grace, as if you reach a certain point with the rest of us and then you go no further. But sometimes you have to give a little more of yourself than is expected. Maybe it's being human. Am I being too blunt with you?"

Grace looked down at her hands, lying tranquilly on the top of the table. They were not betraying her, but actually she was shaking all over inside. What was happening to her—this momentary flush of passion spreading, followed immediately by a cold calculation of the facts as they were: She wanted Harry, but in order to get him she would have to give of herself, give him something that she treasured above and beyond the normal. Was it possible that she was not normal? Could she be frigid? Where did she fit?"

"You didn't answer my question," Maria reminded her. "Was I too blunt with you?"

"Of course not. Perhaps someone should have been blunt with me a long time ago, Maria. Maybe that's one of my troubles."

Maria laughed, and a middle-aged woman at the next table glanced over at them disapprovingly.

"A woman is a woman," Maria said, "and a man is a man. Put the two together and you have what is meant for us."

"Is that what you believe? Truly?"

Maria hesitated, then sighed deeply. "My dear Grace," she said, "I'm not sure what I believe. I know that now you are troubled, that you have met this man, this Harry Mercer, and he is a big thing with you. You are in turmoil, wondering what to do, how to do it, what the consequences will be if—" and she waved a hand, not finishing.

"If what?"

"If nothing. I cannot answer the questions for you. I imagine that is why you asked me to lunch today. You want someone to tell you what to do, how to go about the whole thing. I cannot do that, Grace. I wouldn't if I could."

They were silent while the waitress placed their food before them, and silent while they ate. Grace sat stiffly, wondering why she, of all people, should be apart from everyone else. She had never considered herself in that manner before, but now she believed what Maria had said. She would not give sufficiently of herself, and so, somewhere along the line, she had taken the wrong path, had brought herself to this point of desperation.

Over tea, Maria said, "Each of us is an individual, Grace, and that is as it should be."

Grace looked over the rim of the tea cup at Maria. "You know what Harry is like," she said.

"He is a man who has seen much, perhaps too much for a city like ours, and a man who usually gets what he wants when he wants it."

"He wants me, Maria."

"Any man would be a fool who did not."

Grace was silent for a long moment, and then: "I suppose I did come to you for advice, knowing about you and Jack—"

"What about us?"

She was embarrassed, and she regretted having brought the subject up.

Maria smiled. "You're wondering how I can give myself to a man who is not my husband." Maria looked down. "Well, Grace, a woman is made to be loved, and to love a man. I love Jack, and he loves me. You know the circumstances here in Beach City. Jack wants to marry me; he even begs to marry me. Perhaps, some day, I will weaken enough to consent to this; I'm not sure. My own family is as bigoted in this as are the others, so you can see it is no easy solution for us. But in the meantime we share each other fully, as a man and a woman in love should share each other. I am not ashamed of this and never will be. Perhaps, to some, the fact that we are unmarried yet still share the same bed is wrong. But to us it is right, so very right."

"You're a wonderful woman, Maria," she said.

"Of course I am. Didn't you know?"

They laughed together, but Grace's laughter was on the outside only. She had sought help from two of her friends, and had found solace from neither. Cynthia was twisted, unsure of herself, living a life that was a lie; Maria was going against everything that she believed in, regardless of how she spoke.

Where was the answer?

She took a long and lonely drive after lunch, following the narrow county road that wound around beside the ocean. Later, she stopped at a drugstore and phoned her brother-in-law and asked him to meet her in front of the newspaper office. He was reluctant to do so, but finally agreed.

He was waiting for her when she drove up. Without saying a word, he got into the car, and she drove around to the parking lot and stopped.

"I'm sorry," she said, "about interfering with your day."

"A newspaper doesn't run itself, Grace."

"I know." She hesitated, searching for the right words that would let him know how she felt; this was so important to her. She supposed that, in one way, she was looking on him as a kind of father-image, and that she was now turning to him out of desperation, wanting to get a man's viewpoint.

"We've never been really close, have we, Thomas?"

He was sitting straight, not looking at her. For a moment, she wondered if he had even heard her, and then he said, "That depends on what you mean, Grace. I'm not a person to show my emotions. I admire you, Grace, and I suppose, in a certain way, I feel responsible for you."

"Responsible?"

"Well—you're very young in certain ways." He turned in the seat, looking at her. "Whatever you do has a direct connection with me. Margaret loves you, perhaps a little too possessively to do either of you any good. I love Margaret, so it's that simple."

He seemed so cold-hearted to her then, so matter-of-fact in what he was saying, in the way he was saying it.

"I'm sorry, Thomas," she said. "I won't bother you any more. You can go now."

He smiled. "You've apologized twice now in the last few minutes. Maybe that's my fault. But you don't need

to apologize, Grace. I would like to help you if I could.
I think I know what's bothering you."

"You do?"

"Of course. Let me be completely candid. Harry Mercer is nothing special, Grace, and believe me when I say that. Men like him are a dime a dozen. Maybe you've never known anyone like him before. Your experience has been limited and narrow, Grace—despite your education—and confined, here in Beach City.

"Mercer comes to town and you begin romanticizing him out of all proportion. I know what he wants; I know what they all want. Put him to work on a paper and he'll do an excellent job for you, as he's been doing for me. But all he really wants is enough money to keep him in bottles and women. He drinks hard and he plays hard and all women are the same to him. He wants you in his bed. But you don't want that without being married. Grace, his kind never marries, which means that you're going to have to make up your own mind. Do you want to keep your virginity or do you want this man enough to give that up?"

"How do you know I'm still a virgin?"

He laughed. "Grace, Grace," he said. "Margaret says you are, and that's good enough for me."

"Do you—do you discuss me all the time?"

"Of course we do," he replied without hesitating.

She looked out the car window. It seemed to her that she was on some kind of a merry-go-round, spinning and getting dizzier by the moment, and she wished there was a button that she could press to stop the spinning.

"Is it the man himself you want, Grace?" Thomas asked her kindly. "Or is it the idea of redeeming him from the life he's leading?"

She was silent for a long time, then she said, "I only know that I want to hold him, Thomas, caress him, feel him near me. I can't stop thinking about him, yet I cannot do what he wants me to do. I guess—" and she turned back to him, feeling the tears welling up—"I guess I do have to grow up a little. I can't have my cake and eat it, too, can I? Oh, Thomas!" she blurted reaching for him.

He cradled her head against his shoulder, letting her cry, letting her have this moment of his time. She was so like a small child, searching desperately for she knew not what, and he was thinking that he had two daughters, both of whom would grow and have to face decisions like this in later years. For a moment, he doubted his own wisdom and intelligence, wondering if he and Margaret would be able to guide them properly.

Grace felt secure, almost happy, with her face pressed tightly against Thomas' chest. She let the tears come; she had needed to cry for so long.

eight

AFTER lunch, John Ross sat stiffly in his private office, staring at the mahogany-paneled walls, his hands clasped in his lap. His mind would not organize itself; it was a jumble of confusion at this moment and he searched through it, trying to remember something that was important. He reached over, opened the bottom desk drawer and took out the bottle of bourbon that he kept there. He unscrewed the cap and tipped the bottle to his mouth, downing three large swallows.

At that moment, the door opened and Lynne, his secretary, walked in, a sheaf of papers in her hand. She stopped as she saw what he was doing, then turned and closed the door behind her and came toward him.

"Do you want to sign these now?" she asked, placing the papers on the top of his desk.

"Am I supposed to?"

She smiled, shrugging. "You're the boss," she said.

She was young and quite pretty without being beautiful. Tall and shapely, her dark hair always worn in the latest fashion, she dressed primly and properly. But he had often caught himself looking at her legs. She had been working for him for almost six months, yet he knew almost nothing about her, other than that she was divorced and was the most efficient secretary he had ever had.

He rose to his feet, feeling a wave of dizziness pass through him as he did so. He blinked rapidly.

"Are you okay, Mr. Ross?"

He didn't answer her.

She came around to him quickly, concern in her eyes, her hands raised as if to help him. He could see the soft moistness of her full lips, the whiteness of her teeth. He caught her as she came to him, enveloping her with his arms, drawing her close to him, bringing her face near his. His mouth sought hers, found it; her lips closed tightly, and she stood stiffly against him, neither eager nor protesting, and then he let her go.

"Well! That's the first time you've ever tried anything like that," she said, straightening her dress.

"Should I apologize?"

"I think it might be in order."

"Am I that hard to take?"

She looked at him quickly. "You're not at all hard to take," she said. "But that isn't the point."

"What is the point?"

"Never mind, Mr. Ross. I'm happy the way I am. If you're going to start chasing me around the office, I'll just have to quit."

"You don't have to quit. I won't chase you."

"Is that a promise?"

He shrugged, sitting down again. Damn it, he thought, what was happening to him? He took another long drink from the bottle, set the bottle carefully on the top of his desk. Was that the answer? Could he drink himself into oblivion each day?

"Look," she said, sitting down on the edge of the desk near him, her nylon-sheathed legs crossed, "you're a pretty good guy, Mr. Ross. Everyone here in the office knows about you and your wife, the trouble you're having. I don't listen to office gossip, but I still know what's going on. And that—" and she pointed at the bottle—"certainly won't solve any of your problems."

"What will?"

"That's for you to decide."

He placed a hand on her knee. She did not move, did not try to remove his hand.

"The office is no place for this kind of thing," she said. "Someone might come in that door any moment."

He moved his hand farther up the inside of her leg, felt the smooth, silken texture of her inner thigh, saw the quick change come into her eyes. She moved slightly on the desk, closer to him, bending a little lower so that her face was close to his.

"Kiss me just once," she murmured huskily.

Her lips were willing this time, more than willing; they were demanding and her tongue slipped inside his mouth, burning him with its intensity. His hand wandered further and found what it was seeking, and then she moved off the desk and was bending over him, her own fingers searching, finding him, holding him gently.

And then, almost as suddenly as it had started, it was over and she was moving back away from him, leaving him flushed and excited.

"My God!" she whispered. "I didn't expect that."

He looked down and said, "Are you going to leave me like this?"

She glanced nervously at the door. She seemed to be shaking all over. "We can't, not here," she said.

"To hell with everything."

"No," she said. "No. Don't be like that. I want you. I

want you very much," and she was looking down at him, breathing heavily, her passion evident in her face.

She took a step toward him, then stopped. "Forget it for now, please. Just remember, it's as difficult for me as it is for you."

He rose and stood before her. He had raped his wife; he would not do that to this woman.

"Tonight," she said hurriedly, her voice low, "right after work. You come to my apartment."

"Lynne," was all he could say, and then she had turned and was walking swiftly from the office.

He stood there a moment, fighting down the lust within him, telling himself that it would end this night. He could wait that long; he had to wait that long. He walked slowly around the office, trying his best to calm himself. Her abrupt passion had caught him by surprise, and now he smiled. To hell with Cynthia; he didn't need her. He would divorce her and then everything would be all right. There was just no sense in his treating himself the way he had been doing.

He took another swig from the bottle, put it back in the desk drawer, then walked out of the office. Lynne was sitting at her desk, looking as composed as usual as he walked up to her.

"I'll be back in an hour or so," he said.

A salesman came in with a customer.

Lynne whispered quickly, "Don't forget—tonight," and then, in a louder voice, "All right, Mr. Ross."

He was smiling as he walked out to his car.

The day was suddenly bright and wonderful as he drove toward his home. Everything was going to be fine. Whatever had been bothering him before was now in the past and like a bad dream he could put it aside and forget it. But now he had to tell Cynthia. She had to know that he was going to divorce her, regardless of the cost, regardless of anything...

The house was strangely quiet as he entered. Perhaps

he should have called before coming home; perhaps she had gone out for the afternoon. He felt deprived of his moment of triumph, as if he had been building up to this and now he would not be able to go through with it. Damn her, somehow she managed to rob him of everything.

He went into the kitchen, expecting to find Veline there, but she, too, seemed to have disappeared. Feeling let down, he was turning to leave when he heard a woman's scream from upstairs. He froze in his tracks. The sound had not been one of fright; rather, it was the sound of pure ecstasy, and he stood there a moment longer before he turned swiftly toward the stairs.

When he reached the bedroom door, he saw them, their nude bodies gleaming with perspiration, entangled together in an unnatural position. She was getting what she wanted now, he thought. He felt strangely elated and was backing out of the door when he saw that the man with her, Carl Morris, had seen him. He whirled and half-ran, half-stumbled down the hallway, down the stairs. He went directly to his den and to his desk. His mind was crystal-clear; he knew exactly what he was going to do and he almost laughed as he jerked open the desk drawer where he kept his .38 revolver. He hastily checked the weapon; it was loaded.

"Good," he said aloud. "Very good."

He walked quickly back upstairs. He felt as if he had grown several inches within the past few moments. He paused a moment outside the bedroom door, breathing deeply, feeling a wave of self-pity that he would be unable to keep his date with Lynne. She had been so eager in her passion and had promised so much, and now that promise would never be fulfilled. Too bad, he thought, he would have liked to have known her.

At that point, he opened the bedroom door and unhurriedly walked inside.

Morris was standing by the bed, wearing only a T-shirt. John looked at him for a silent moment, wondering what sort of man this was; he looked like any ordinary man, nothing special, yet he had been able to take Cynthia from him. Cynthia abruptly rose from the bed and stood beside Morris.

"Look," Morris started, "let's not act like a couple of animals now. She asked me here, and I came."

"Of course," John said.

Cynthia was frowning, looking at him intently. "Hell, Carl," she said a little angrily, "don't waste your breath. He's not man enough to do anything."

"This is my mother's house," John said, taking the revolver from his coat pocket, pointing it at them. "You could have had the courtesy to do your filth elsewhere."

Morris backed away a step, his hands raised before him, ice-cold fright in his eyes. "My God, man," he whispered. "Put that thing away."

"John," Cynthia said disdainfully. "Don't be a damned idiot."

He pulled the trigger once, heard the gun's flat noise and saw Morris's body jerk around. Morris flopped on the bed, then slowly slid off until he was half-sitting, half-lying against the foot of the bed. Blood spurted from his chest and his hands were folded together over the wound, trying to stem the crimson flow. John pulled the trigger a second time and heard Cynthia's high-pitched screech as Morris's face seemed to dissolve into a bloody mass with the impact of the bullet.

He turned to her. She went down on her knees. "Please, John," she begged. "Oh, please, please, please—"

He laughed, pulling the trigger twice, watching her body collapse to the floor as the bullets struck her. She looked pitiful there, small, helpless and forgotten, and he fired a third time at her just to make sure. A pool of dark blood seeped from beneath her crumpled body, glistening on the Chinese Oriental rug where she lay, so limp and unknowing.

John muttered, "I'm sorry, Mother, about the carpet."

He put the barrel of the revolver in his mouth, looked up at the ceiling for a moment. This was it; this was how it was going to end, and there was nothing he could do about it, nothing he really wished to do. He pulled the trigger again.

Thomas Hennings carefully put down the phone. For the first time in a long while, he felt numbed with shock. He sat there a moment, sorting out his thoughts, arranging in his mind the story he had just heard. How could a solid citizen like John Ross have gotten himself involved in such a situation? The police reporter had called him immediately, giving him the facts of the story, and now Hennings must decide how to run that story, how to treat it, to evaluate it. He shook his head. John Ross and Cynthia. The reporter had been explicit in the details.

He sighed and leaned back in his chair. He was a man who liked his life to go along smoothly, with no jumps or jerks to interrupt his carefully planned placidity. Recently that placidity had been harshly disturbed by two events: the first, of course, was the arrival of Harry Mercer in to Beach City and his subsequent emotional effect on Grace; and the second was the double murder and suicide. There was neither rhyme nor reason when a man like John Ross did something like this. Hennings knew, of course, that he could subdue the story even if he could not suppress it. The tragic event would have to appear in the paper, but he could alter the facts sufficiently to hide what had really happened. John Ross had been a member of Hennings' group, which meant that, even now, he deserved some kind of protection, and Hennings would see that he got it.

Well, it was too late to get the story into today's editions. Time enough for that tomorrow. He looked around as his office door opened and Mercer entered.

"You busy?"

"What's on your mind?"

"I just heard about John Ross," Harry said. "How are you going to play the story, Mr. Hennings?"

"I think that doesn't concern you in your present assignment," he answered stiffly. And then: "I'm not just sure, Mercer. The Rosses were friends of mine, and I just heard about it myself. Anyhow, it's general news and you're off that temporarily, remember?"

"I'd like to use it in my series."

"Why?"

"It's a part of Beach City, isn't it? John and Cynthia Ross were highly respected members of the community. They've had their pictures in the society section time and again. They're news, Mr. Hennings, and I'd like to be able to—"

"Leave it alone, Mercer!"

Harry's eyes narrowed. He leaned forward on the balls of his feet, his mouth drawn tight. "In other words—"

"In other words, nothing," Hennings broke in. "You work for me and I'm telling you to leave it alone. That's an order. If you don't like it, quit."

Harry turned and stamped out of the office. Hennings watched him walk right through the city room and out the back. The man had not answered him, and he wondered if he had quit or was just going some place to cool off for a while. Probably he would get drunk; his kind always did. Whatever could Grace, with all her intelligence and education, see in a man like that? Hennings remembered how she had lain against his shoulder, crying and sobbing, and a moment of tenderness touched him.

He knew instinctively what Mercer would want to do with the Ross story and Hennings also knew that he wouldn't let Mercer do it. Hennings shook his head, annoyed. It seemed that his whole world had been turned topsy-turvy since Mercer had come to Beach City. Of course, Hennings told himself, he could not blame the Ross shooting on Mercer, yet Hennings thought how convenient it would be if just such a thing were possible.

His phone rang, and he answered. "Thomas," his wife's voice said immediately. "I just heard the news on the radio. It's horrible."

"I know," he said.

"Is it true?"

"I'm afraid it is."

"They gave no details, just that John had shot and killed Cynthia and that Carl Morris and then killed himself. Oh, I knew something like this was going to happen—I just knew it!"

"Take it easy, Margaret. I'll see that nothing distasteful gets in the paper."

"What really happened, Thomas?"

"I'd—rather tell you in private."

"That bad?"

"It couldn't be worse."

He sat there after hanging up the phone. He would protect John Ross; he had to protect him.

But what he was really worrying about was Harry Mercer. The man was like a slow-burning fuse, and he wished he could foresee how Mercer would react to this.

nine

HARRY lay awkwardly, his feet extending over the end of the couch, his hands cupped beneath his head. He was listening to the soft sounds of the symphony coming from the hi-fi in the corner. He turned his head as Bess came into the room, watching her take a chair opposite him. She looked cool and comfortable in a pink cotton, her tanned, shapely legs bare, her feet in white sandals. She sighed, lit a cigarette and blew the smoke away.

"You look too damned contented for my money," she said.

"It's a man's world, Bess."

"Don't I know that?"

"You should, by now."

"No comments on the dinner?"

"It was wonderful. It was the most. It was absolutely the greatest meal I've had in the past two days." He smiled across at her, winking. "You have certain talents, lady, but I don't think they include any art in the kitchen department."

"What talents do I have?"

"Are you kidding?"

"Of course not."

He sat up, searching for a cigarette in the box on the coffee table. He lit the cigarette, staring at her through the smoke.

"Your one obvious and foremost talent is that you're positively the best bed performer these tired old bones have ever experienced."

"I suppose I should thank you for that," she said, not looking at him. "You've obviously had plenty of experience, so you should be an authority on the subject."

"Bully for you."

"I am. I admit it."

"I said the wrong thing, didn't I?"

She stubbed out her cigarette, ran both hands down along her thighs, smoothing her dress down, not answering.

"What's wrong, Bess?" he asked.

"I don't know. I feel—funny. That's not a good word, but it's the only one I can think of at the moment.

You know, this is the first time we've been together alone for more than ten minutes when we haven't hopped right into bed."

"You want that now?"

"No."

"Honest-Injun?"

She laughed. "Honestly, Harry, sometimes you're exactly like a small boy."

He, too, laughed. "Part of my charm."

They were silent for a moment and he sucked on his cigarette, wondering why he had run to her after leaving Hennings.

She had been the first person to enter his mind, and he had not even bothered calling, he had just hopped in his car and driven here. She had asked no questions; she had given him a peck on the cheek and asked him to stay for dinner. She had fixed him the best martini he had had in months and then had gone to a lot of trouble trying to make a passable meal for him, and now he was being rude to her. He wished that he could understand himself, why he was acting the way he was toward her. She certainly deserved better.

He got up and, without another word to her, left the house. He got in his car and drove around until he found a small flower shop that was still open. He bought a bouquet of red roses and drove back to Bess's house.

She seemed not to have moved the entire time he had been gone. She looked up at him, and her eyes flickered with something he could not read when she saw the roses.

"A peace offering," he said. "From a naughty little boy with a nasty mouth."

She took the flowers from him, looked at them and then at him for a moment, then suddenly burst into tears and ran from the room.

He stood there, running one hand through his hair, wondering what in hell he had done wrong this time. He just couldn't figure it, and he damned himself for being stupid.

As he was turning to leave, Bess came back into the room. She had put the flowers in a green glass vase which she placed on the mantel before turning to look at him. Her eyes were red-rimmed and her hands were nervously clenched before her.

"You make it awfully tough on a girl," she said.

"How so?"

"Never mind, Harry."

He went to her and held her close. He was puzzled by his feelings toward her and unsure of himself. He looked down at her, tipping her chin up with his fingers, kissing her lightly on the lips.

"You've never kissed me like that before," she said.

He led her to the couch and they sat down beside each other, his arm around her shoulders, snuggling her against him. He felt peaceful and contented, and some of the drive and tension went from his body. Perhaps this was the other side of the coin, the non-sexual side, the times when a man and a woman could sit beside each other and just enjoy each other's company. The thought that this woman next to him might be coming to mean too much to him suddenly frightened him, and he had a sudden blind impulse to get up and run. All this time he had been worrying about Grace, and instead, maybe he should have been worrying about Bess.

"I've—never been so happy," she said, breaking the silence. "No one has brought me flowers in—well, longer than I care to admit."

"You know, I think that's the first bouquet I've ever given to a girl."

"I'm not a girl, Harry. I'm a woman."

"Yes," he said, looking gravely at her, "you are a woman. And there is a difference."

"I think I'm in love with you."

He shook his head. "Don't be."

"I can't help it, Harry."

His hand squeezed her shoulder. "Now you're making it tough for me."

"I'm not asking anything from you. I just wanted you to know." She brought her mouth up to his, kissed him gently. Her fingers traced a path down his cheek. "I won't fight you, Harry. When you want to leave, just pick up your bags and go."

They were interrupted by the phone ringing. Bess hesitated. "I don't want to answer it," she said.

"You'd better."

She rose and went to the phone. A puzzled look came on her face as she answered then she turned to Harry and said, "It's for you."

He took the phone. "Yes?"

"Are you still working for me or did you quit?" the voice of Thomas Hennings asked him abruptly.

"I'm still working for you."

"Good. There's been a knifing down in the Mexican section. I want you to cover it."

"Why not the regular police reporter?"

"I told you what I wanted, Mercer. Now get on it."

The phone was slammed down in his ear.

He stood there a moment, staring at the phone, then slowly replaced it and turned to Bess. "I guess I've got to go," he said. "That was my dear little boss and I have to cover a story."

"How did he know you were here?"

He shrugged. He didn't want to leave. Momentarily, he thought of calling Hennings back, of telling him that he was actually going to quit. And then he thought better of that. He was, first and foremost, a reporter, and this was a story.

"I'm sorry, Bess," he said.

She kissed him quickly. "I'll see you later."

"Of course."

A tired-looking little fat man sat in a straight-backed chair in one corner, occupied in cleaning his fingernails. From outside the small office could be heard the sounds of men talking in the hallway. The fat man looked over at Harry, grinned, showing two front upper teeth missing and said, "Ain't seen you around here before."

Harry did not bother to answer. He sat slumped in a chair, his feet up on the desk, his hands stuffed in his coat pockets. He had the definite feeling that he was being given the old run-around, as if no one gave a damn whether or not he found out what was going on. He had been at the police station for almost a half an hour now, and had learned absolutely nothing.

The door opened and a stocky, gray-haired policeman, wearing a sergeant's chevrons, entered. He glanced at Harry, then at the fat man, and asked, "You still here, Bobo?"

"I got to see the lieutenant," the fat man said.

"He's busy. Get out."

"But I—"

"Get out, Bobo!"

The fat man made a sound with his lips but at another look from the sergeant, rose quickly and left the room.

"That damned whining bastard spends half his time in here," the sergeant said.

"For what reason?"

"You tell me and then we'll both know." He searched through his pockets, finally finding the stub of a cigar, stuck the stub in his mouth and began chewing on it. "You Mercer?"

"That's right."

"How come you're handling this and not Scott?"

"Because Hennings pays my salary and he told me to get my tail down here. Any other questions?"

The sergeant grinned, shifting the cigar from one side of his mouth to the other.

"The desk told me Lieutenant Skinner was in charge of the case," Harry said.

"He's busy now. He sent me along. What you want to know?"

"Everything."

"Okay." The sergeant slumped into the chair vacated by the fat man. "It's open and shut; nothing left to figure out but the charge. Three guys jumped two others downtown. One of the guys that did the jumping pulled a knife and stuck it in where it hurts. The guy stuck is in City Hospital, hanging on God only knows how. The medics give him a fifty-fifty chance. We got five eyewitnesses saw the whole thing, but none of 'em knows which one did the sticking."

Harry sighed, removing his feet from the desk, sitting up, rubbing a hand across his eyes. This sergeant was going to be a lot of help. The way he told the story meant absolutely nothing.

"Juvenile delinquency?" Harry asked.

"What's that?"

"You're funny, you are."

"I'm a riot," the sergeant said. "I get my four-seventy-six a month, less everything they take out, and you want me to be funny and tell you a big story about juvenile delinquency. I never heard of such a thing. A guy commits a crime, to me it don't matter whether he's fifteen or fifty."

Harry glanced at the large clock on one wall. Almost eleven-thirty. He'd have to hustle to get everything down for the first edition.

"Could I see the booking sheet?" he asked.

"Why not?"

Harry followed the sergeant from the small room, down the long hallway and into another room where he was told to wait. It was the first room all over again, the two chairs, the desk, the clock on the wall. Harry lit a cigarette, failed to see an ashtray and dropped the used match to the floor. He waited five minutes, then ten, and finally the sergeant returned with the booking sheet which he handed to Harry.

Harry glanced through the record. It was simple and to the point. There seemed to be neither sense nor reason to the crime so far as Harry could see; nothing, apparently, had caused it, and this set him to wondering about it. He copied the names of the three who had done the attacking: Carlos Mendez, Raul Guerrero, and Manuel Sanfilippo. Carlos and Raul were both twenty-two; Manuel was nineteen. Floyd Clayton, sixteen, was the boy who had been stabbed and was hospitalized and near death. The other one, severely beaten but not critically so, was named Melvin Duncan, seventeen. The eyewitnesses all seemed to be reputable, solid citizens. According to them, a car containing the three Mexican youths had pulled up alongside Clayton and Duncan around ten o'clock that night. The latter two had been standing outside a movie theater where the three Mexicans had assaulted them. None of the witnesses could identify which of the three had done the knifing.

"Simple, ain't it?" the sergeant asked.

"But why?"

"Why what?"

"Why was it done?"

"You a kook or something, Mercer?" The sergeant looked at him as if he had just arrived from another planet. "That ain't in my department. I don't give a damn about why. We know one of 'em did it, and that's enough for us. What else is there?"

Before Harry could answer, the door opened, and a tall, thin man in his early forties entered. He had a long nose and drooping eyelids and a faint scar along the right side of his face. He glanced curiously at Harry.

"You fill him in?" he asked the sergeant.

"He's one of those nuts wants to know why."

"How come you're handling this, Mercer?"

"You must be Lieutenant Skinner?"

"Who in hell you think I am? Santa Claus?"

The sergeant laughed, and Skinner grinned ruthlessly.

"Look, Lieutenant," Harry said, "I'm only doing my job. All I know is that my boss assigned this to me and I've been getting the run-around for the past hour or so and I'm getting damned sick and tired of it."

"You're real rough and tough," Skinner said.

"I can be."

Skinner waved a hand in the direction of the sergeant, who immediately rose and left the room.

"Okay, Mercer," Skinner said. "Here's the way it is. I'm surprised Hennings or Scott didn't fill you in before. We got a nice clean little town here and we like to keep it that way. We usually keep people like these bundled up in their own part of town. Tonight, we goofed and these three bastards got out and made a rupture in the wrong part of town. I'm damned mad about it and I don't care who knows it.

"I know Hennings. I know the way he likes things, and me and him see eye-to-eye on things like this. So don't get tough with me or I'll have you fired and roasted and outa here in less time than you can blink an eye."

"You're a pretty hard guy, Lieutenant."

"I eat nails for breakfast."

"I believe you."

Skinner pulled at his lower lip. "You write it the way I tell it to you and Hennings will go along with it." He glanced up at the clock, then back at Harry. "The case is all wrapped up, and it's just a matter of the charge now. If the Clayton kid dies, it'll be first-degree murder. We can't close our eyes to things like this—"

"No one's asking you to do that."

"—and I'm going to make damned sure," Skinner went on, "mighty damned sure. They need a lesson down in that part of town, and they're going to get one."

Harry was shocked by Skinner's biased attitude, but

he kept his thoughts to himself. He asked if he could see the three youths.

Skinner said, "Why not?"

He was led to an interrogation room and, shortly, two uniformed policemen led the three youths inside. They were what Harry had expected, young and tough, angry at the world, hiding their fears beneath a thin veneer of bad humor. Mendez was the obvious leader.

"You gonna write this up, huh?" Mendez asked him.

"Of course I am."

"Make sure you spell my name right," Guerrero put in.

"Look, mister, we know the score," Mendez said, glancing at the two uniformed policemen. "Who you tryin' to kid?"

"I'm not trying to kid anyone. I thought I might get your side of the story, that's all."

Mendez and Guerrero gave a sneering laugh, while Sanfilippo nervously rubbed his hands together.

"The police know," Sanfilippo said.

"Know what?" Harry prodded him.

"Ah, what's the use, Manuel?" Mendez asked.

Harry could get nothing more from them.

Unhappy with what he had learned, knowing that he could not write a decent story with the material he had, Harry nevertheless went back to the office and started to write for the next day's early editions. He read the story through when he had finished, and it was bad and he knew it was bad. There was something lacking in it, some element of the truth that he could not reach. What was it that the police knew? What was the reason for this seemingly senseless crime? He phoned the hospital for a report on the Clayton boy, found that the kid's chances were still listed at fifty-fifty.

Harry was sitting slumped at his desk, smoking a cigarette in the deserted city room, when he heard someone approaching from behind. He whirled around and saw Grace coming toward him.

"You like this place, don't you?" she said by way of greeting him. "You like sitting here all alone."

"What are you doing here?" He glanced at his watch. It was almost two-thirty in the morning. "You should be home in that lonely bed of yours."

"Don't be smart with me, Harry," she said.

She sat down in a chair next to his desk. She seemed tired and drawn and he felt a brief touch of compassion for her.

"What are you doing here?" he asked again.

"I'm not sure. I heard about what happened—the knifing, I mean—and I called Thomas."

"I thought he was always in bed by a certain time."

She smiled wanly. "He wasn't too happy about my waking him. But he said you were on the story."

"Grace, why don't you go home? I'm bushed. I've had a long day and things aren't adding up for me and I'd like to be alone to sort out my thoughts on this thing."

"I could help you with the story."

He had to laugh at that.

"No, really," she insisted. "I've been working with a committee for some time, trying to break through the barrier separating those poor people who live in that section of town from the rest of us. There are so many things that could be done for them, if they would only let someone help."

"Maybe they'd like to help themselves."

She ignored that. "At times, I've felt as if they like to be what they are; they like living amid their poverty. I don't know, Harry, I really don't."

He was staring at her. She really was breathtakingly beautiful, one of those rare women set apart from the common lot. She possessed that kind of beauty that enveloped everything and everyone around her, and he tried to picture her working with a committee down there, trying to help those less fortunate than herself. He almost laughed. He could see the men and the boys down there, looking at her, making remarks behind her back.

"I—I know one of the boys involved," she said. "Manuel Sanfilippo. He's a good boy, Harry, a very good boy. I know his sister, Angelina, too. They're both nice people, and I'm sure there must be some kind of a mistake in his case."

"Five responsible citizens say that he was one of them."

"I still can't believe it."

"And the other two?"

She shook her head, lifted a hand in his direction and for a moment he thought she was going to touch him, then she dropped her hand.

"They're simply products of their environment," she said. "I suppose all of us are at fault in something like this. We keep them down there, even though some of us don't like the situation."

Something about her attitude bothered him. He got the idea that she was trying to solve some personal problem by helping those less fortunate than herself; he wondered if she actually understood them, tried to understand them, or if she just gave a little time and effort to something she really did not believe in. But perhaps he was being too rough on her.

"Well," he said, "I've had it for one night."

"Drive me home, Harry. Please."

He looked at her, then slowly nodded. He dropped his copy on the city editor's desk, then walked with her down to his car. They were silent during the drive and when he drew up before her house she made no effort to get out.

"Thomas called me earlier tonight," she said. "He wanted to know if you were with me."

"And you told him I was probably with Bess Higgins?"

"Yes." She turned from him in the seat; he could not

see her in the dimness of the dash light. Suddenly she said, "Why, Harry?"

"Why what?"

"Why do you—spend so much time with her?"

"That's a damned stupid question and, besides, it's none of your business."

"She isn't for you, Harry."

"No woman is for me."

"I could be."

He wished he could see her more clearly; she was leaning toward him now and her features were only a vague blur. He wished he could read what was in her eyes.

"That's nonsense," he said.

"Harry?"

"You'd better go in, Grace."

"I don't want to go in. Not yet."

"No, I know what you want. You want to sit here with me and gab until I make a pass at you. You'll let me go so far, get me all heated up, and then you'll say night-night dear Harry, and run in the house. No, thanks."

"It won't always be like that," she said.

He felt the slow pulse of his heart beating. He did not want to go through this with her again; he knew what the ending would be, and he did not want that. Her fingers strayed against his face, ran quickly, tantalizingly, across his lips. He reached for her, pulling her to him. Their mouths met, clung together. Her lips tasted wonderfully sweet. Her hands were cupped on either side of his face. He opened his mouth and was surprised when she slid her tongue inside. He felt the heat rising within him, the hard shock of his rising passion.

Her fingers stole down, unbuttoning his shirt, then slipping inside against his flesh. He felt her fingers move across his chest, and then they came up for air, their faces still so close together that he could feel the heat of her breath against him.

"You're so strong, Harry," she whispered. "Are you—do you—want me?"

"Damn!" he snapped. "What do you think?"

"Kiss me again, the way you just did."

Their mouths met. He was throbbing with passion now and he forced her back against the seat. Her hand had moved again, this time farther down. She was groping, unsure of herself, and then she was holding him, a little too hard, and he wanted to tell her to stop, and did not.

She moved her mouth from his, yet still clung to him as his hands moved inside her dress, pushing down her brassiere. He enveloped the warm fullness of her ripe breasts in his hands, feeling the nipples harden into twin pinnacles of desire.

"Oh, God, Harry! Oh, God!" she moaned between clenched teeth. You'd hurt me so—"

"I won't hurt you."

"Please, Harry." She removed her hand.

He could not believe that she could go this far only to back down. He bent his head and put his lips around one of her nipples. It seemed almost to burn inside of his mouth. She pulled his head away.

He turned from her, his emotions jangled and upset. He wanted to strike out at something, anything, yet he only sat there and tried to gain control of himself, tried not to let her know how she had managed to get him so upset.

She kissed his cheek. "We went further this time."

"I guess," he said, trying to keep his voice normal, "that must be some consolation. To someone."

"The next time—"

"There'll be no next time."

"I love you, Harry."

He laughed. "You don't know what love is, damn you! I tasted the sweetness of you and I wanted you and you had gone so far with me and that was all, and now you sit there and tell me that you love me. What kind of a crazy woman are you?"

"Please don't use such language, Harry."

"Get out! Get away from me!"

"It takes time, Harry. I have to get—"

He reached across her, opening the door on her side.

She touched his face with her fingers. "You're angry with me," she said.

"Good God in Heaven. What do you expect me to be?"

She made no reply, sitting like a small stone statue, immovable, unresponsive. He damned the day he had met her, damned her for being so beautiful and tantalizing, damned her for being what she was. He had come from a good, whole woman like Bess Higgins to one like this, and he was wondering what madness had possessed him to let him do such a thing.

"Harry, if I—if I let you come in, will you—will you be tender with me? Will you not hurt me? I couldn't stand to be hurt."

She needed someone wiser than he was, he decided, someone less self-centered, someone who could devote his whole being, his whole soul, just to her, just to making her happy, keeping up with her whims and her moods.

"I'm not coming in now, Grace. Please, just go now. Do that much for me."

She stared at him from the darkness, and then she was out of the car, closing the door. He could see the outline of her figure standing on the curb and, momentarily, he wondered if he was making a mistake; this could be the time, he told himself and she would be the most beautiful and desirable woman he would ever possess. And yet he could not go into the house with her, could not let himself be led any further into nothing but torment.

He gunned the car away from the curb.

He could take only so much, and he had reached the end.

ten

AT last, Bess answered his insistent ringing of the door-bell. She blinked the sleep from her eyes, staring out at him. She was wearing a thin, transparent nightgown, through which he could see the softly rounded lines of her voluptuous body, the inviting globes of her breasts with their coral-colored tips showing dark in the shadow.

"It's after four in the morning," she said sleepily. "Are you doubling for the milkman?"

"If you answer the door like this, I'll be your personal, full-time milkman, lady, every day of the year.

She made a sound like laughter. "I knew it would be you."

"You look damned delicious to me."

"Well, are you going to stand out there and yak all the rest of the night or are you coming inside?"

He laughed, moving inside, slamming the door behind him. He swept her up in his arms, cradling her close to him, burying his face in the soft lushness of her full breasts. She nibbled at the lobe of his ear and he felt, once again, the full rush of his passion. He carried her into the bedroom and by the time he had undressed she was lying nude and waiting for him.

"I'd like the light on," she said huskily. "I want to see you. I want to watch those eyes of yours change color."

He hesitated a moment. Guilt touched him, stayed with him, and he turned from the bed and pounded a closed fist against the wall. He felt helpless and alone; he did not want to take advantage of her this way and yet he could not seem to help himself. For the first time in longer than he could remember, he was in over his head, groping through a situation that he couldn't understand.

"What is it, Harry?" she asked him.

"I've been with Grace." He was shocked at the sound of his voice.

"I think I knew that."

He turned, looking at her. "And you still want me?"

"I'd want you no matter what, Harry. Don't you understand that?"

He bounded over to her, falling into the warm circle of her arms and legs, burying his mouth against hers, letting his pulsating rhythm match hers, and everything seemed good and fine . . .

The sun winked brightly through the half-opened drapes of the bedroom. He turned his head and saw that the bedside lamp was still burning. Bess lay beside him, the even cadence of her breathing telling him that she was still asleep. He looked down at her, at the warm and wonderful beauty of this woman, and he thought of how it would be to awaken beside her each morning for the rest of his life. Had he fallen in love with her? Was that possible for him? Had cynical, worldly Harry Mercer finally gone off the deep end? All these years of chasing and then running away at the last moment, and now there could be an end to them, a hopeful end.

She lay on her side, her legs drawn up slightly, one arm thrown across his chest in a careless gesture of possession.

Well, why not? Why shouldn't she possess him? Her face was half-buried in a pillow and he could see only one eye. As he looked at her, that one eye opened and stared back at him and he saw the slow crinkles of a smile form around that eye and at the corner of her mouth. She rolled over on her back. Her breasts were

large but they remained firm and upright. Her reddish
hair lay spread out on the pillow.

"Good morning," she said.

"Good morning."

"I must look a mess."

Her lips were slightly puffy from the pressure of his
mouth against them. He placed a finger on them tenderly.

"You're beautiful," he said, "the most beautiful woman
I've seen since I was nine years old and violently in love
with the mother of a friend of mine."

"I hope you didn't do the same things with her that
you've been doing with me. Not at that age."

"I'm no cad. I don't gossip about my cast-off sweet-
hearts."

She laughed. "I thought I might have dreamed last
night," she said. "I heard the doorbell ring and there
you were, and you swept me up in your arms, and—"

"And a good time was had by all." He hesitated; he
wanted to say more, so much more, and yet the words
seemed beyond him.

He rose from the bed and went into the bathroom,
rinsing his face and hands in cold water. He stared at
his reflection in the mirror, running his hands through
his hair. When he came back out, she had put on a
flowered housecoat, demurely buttoned to her throat. She
was brushing her hair.

"You shock me, Mr. Mercer," she said, "running around
a woman's house nude like that. What would the neigh-
bors think?"

He was nervous; he was more nervous than he had
ever been before. Nothing had ever happened to him like
this. He knew then that he was in love with this woman,
that he wanted to share the rest of his life with her. He
looked down at his hands; they were shaking.

"What's wrong, Harry?" she asked quickly, concern in
her tone.

"Nothing. It's—nothing."

"You've got a sort of shocked look on your face."

"I've just discovered something, Bess, something I never thought I would discover." He looked carefully into her eyes. "I—I'm in love with you. Don't ask me how it happened, or when or why."

She put a hand to her mouth and her eyes widened. She seemed to sway before him, and then she leaned back against her dresser.

"Harry, don't play with me. Please don't."

"I'm not playing with you, Bess."

"You mean it, actually?"

"I mean it, Bess. I want to marry you."

She turned away from him, hunching her shoulders up. He heard the sound of her crying, and he went to her, placing his hands gently on her shoulders, turning her to face him, tilting her chin up to his gaze. The tears were streaming down her cheeks and her lower lip was quivering.

"I love you, Bess."

"Oh, Harry," she said, and threw her arms around him, holding him tightly.

They stood that way for a long moment, and then she backed away from him. "Harry, my darling," she said, "I've failed twice before. Doesn't that frighten you?"

"The only thing that frightens me is not being with you."

She laughed. She whirled around in a mock dance before him, laughing like a small girl who has just discovered an amazing secret.

"You're beautiful and amazing," he said.

"Just keep saying that."

"You're beautiful, beautiful, beautiful."

She danced into his arms, hugged him closely, reached up to kiss him on the mouth, then danced away again.

"I'm going to fix you the damndest breakfast any man ever had," she said. "You get in there and take a shower and get dressed, and then come out into the kitchen."

"Are you going to give me orders all the time?"

"Just this once, my darling man. My darling, darling man."

Harry did as he was told and, for once, he didn't object to it. He even found a razor—with a dull blade—and hacked away the stubble of his morning beard. He felt like a new man, a man suddenly aware of the shining wonder of life when he entered the kitchen. Bess had not been joking about the breakfast; there were waffles and fried eggs and link sausage and crisp bacon and orange juice and steaming cups of coffee and, when he finally finished, he felt like a balloon about to take off into space.

"If you fix many more meals like that," he said, "I'll have to be hoisted in and out of bed."

"I'll attend to that," she said happily.

Over cigarettes and a final cup of coffee, he told her about the knifing on the previous night, of his helpless feeling about the whole situation. "There's nothing I can do about it, Bess," he said, "absolutely nothing. I know there's more to this than I've been able to discover. But no one on either side seems to give a good damn about what has happened. No one even questions it. The police, I'm sure, are hiding something. The three Mexican boys don't seem to care whether they live or die. I can't understand any of it. Maybe I've been out of this country too long, living abroad. Maybe my values have changed."

"No one wants to understand any of it," Bess said. "You'll find yourself nothing but trouble if you try and dig into this story, Harry. Take it for what it appears to be and write the story the way Hennings wants it, and let it go at that."

"Do you really mean that?"

"No," she replied, "of course I don't, but I still had to say it. I've been mesmerized by being a part of this city, Harry. I grew up here and maybe I should think the way people like Thomas Hennings want me to think. But by golly, I've never been able to conform."

"I'm glad of that."

"You know, I think I've finally figured you out. I know what makes you tick, underneath that hard outer shell. You're the kind who goes around sticking his nose right in the middle of tender subjects, stirring up trouble for the ostrich-type people who like to dream with their heads in the nice, warm sand—for all those who don't give a damn and just want to be left alone—people like me."

But he knew that Bess did give a damn, and much more.

Harry was conscious of the stares focused on him as he walked into the city room. He saw Henry Grayson, the city editor, sitting in Hennings' office.

Hennings' face held a scowl of anger. Grayson, a hard-muscled little man with sad, hound-dog eyes and a ridiculous mustache, stared at his fingertips.

"What kind of a story was that you thought you left on Grayson's desk last night?" Hennings asked angrily.

"It wasn't last night; it was this morning." No matter what provocation they gave him, he told himself that he would not get angry. He did not want to go into this halfcocked. "I spent a lot of time down at the police station. I even talked to Lieutenant Skinner, a fine, up-standing citizen, a real Marshal Dillon lawman, protecting the rights of the individual in this fair city. I wrote what I felt."

Grayson coughed nervously.

"Tell him what we did with his story, Henry," Hennings said.

"We filed it in the waste basket," Grayson answered dutifully, as if repeating something learned by rote.

Hennings rose, placing his hands on his hips, staring across at Harry. He looked something like an enraged elementary school teacher ready to dress down an in-subordinate student.

"I put you on that story for one good reason," Hennings said. "I wanted you to see the other side of life

here in Beach City, the kind of life that the rest of us
have to put up with every day of the year. Those people
down there are nothing but trouble-makers—always have
been and always will be. And you had the brassbound
gall to write a story—" his face turned a shade darker
and he waved a hand in the air— "like that, a story that
said maybe there were two sides to this."

"Maybe there are," he said.

"Are you crazy, Mercer, or just plain stupid? I'm not
sure any more. Five eyewitnesses saw those three jump
out of the car and attack those two helpless boys, boys
from good families, boys from families that make this
city what it is."

"But what caused it? Why did they do it?"

"Who knows why scum like them do anything?"

"I thought you were running a newspaper here. I
thought maybe you'd like a little truth in the story. I'm
sure the police are withholding something."

"Prove it!"

"I can't. Not right now."

"You're a fool, Mercer."

"Perhaps." Harry was having a hard time keeping himself under control. He wanted to lash out at this man,
to hit him where it would hurt. Grayson sat with his head
bowed; it was as if he were some place else, some place
far away. Perhaps, Harry reflected, the man did have a
conscience after all, if only in vestigial form.

"I'm giving you one more chance, Mercer, and that's
the end," Hennings said, threatening. "I'm not fooling
with you this time. I personally rewrote your lead story
this morning. Now I want a follow-up from you for tomorrow's editions. And in it, I want the facts listed as they
exist. Do I make myself clear?"

"You want a story parroting what you think and what
the police told me. Is that it?"

"I want that story at my house tonight, no later than
six o'clock."

Harry bowed from the waist. "Yes, sir, Mr. Hennings. Anything you say, Mr. Hennings, sir."

He was tight inside with anger as he marched out of Hennings' office. He had never taken guff like that from anyone and wanted above all else to go back there and stuff the story right into Hennings' big mouth. But he realized that would serve no useful purpose. Besides already the inkling of an idea was starting to take shape in the back of his mind.

He went to his hotel to change clothes. While he was changing, Bess called him on the phone "I tried your office and they said you'd left. How did it go?"

"They chucked out my first story," he answered. "The old man has given me until tonight to come up with a follow-up."

"Written the way he wants it, I suppose."

"Of course."

He heard the gentle sound of her laughter. "I miss you."

"Still love me?"

"Come over here and I'll show you how much."

"I couldn't do a damned thing right now, honey," he said. "My waist-line expanded five inches with that breakfast. You're going to have to wait another week."

"I wouldn't bet on that."

"Neither would I."

She hesitated. He could hear the muffled sound of her voice as she talked with someone. And then: "I called you for a purpose, Harry. My cleaning woman is here now. Do you want to know the real reason those three jumped the other two boys?"

"Of course."

"You'll be bucking city hall, darling. You can't win, remember?"

"You'd be mighty damn surprised at what I can do."

"All right, it's your funeral. She tells me that those two boys from the good families had followed Angelina

Sanfilippo—Manuel's sister—earlier in the evening, making obscene remarks to her. They dragged her in their car and tried to rape her, though they didn't go through with that part of it."

"Are you sure about this?"

"As sure as I am about anything."

"Why are you telling me?"

She said, laughing, "Maybe I'd like to see you with a bloody head, like the rest of us peasants."

He was grinning as he replaced the phone. He stood there a moment, sorting through his thoughts, then picked up the phone again. He put through a person-to-person call to an old friend of his in New York, an associate editor on a national pictorial magazine with headquarters in the midtown area.

"Harry, you old bastard, what are you doing out there in the land of oranges and sunshine? Come back and suffer with the rest of us."

Harry gave it to him quickly—what he thought about the story that was unfolding in Beach City, how the police were covering up what had really happened, and then asked, "Would you be interested in an article for the magazine?"

"If you can back up what you say with proof, sure."

"I'll keep in touch."

"Do that, Harry."

eleven

ANGELINA SANFILIPPO was seventeen years old, a quiet and subdued young girl who radiated a subtle kind of Latin beauty. She wore her dark hair pulled straight back, a bun at the nape of her neck. She was wearing a demure light-gray dress with a white collar at her throat, and now she sat with her hands folded in her lap, her dark-brown eyes staring straight at Harry.

He could hear the sound of a motorcycle speeding up the street outside and someone in the building shouted in Mexican. The blinds were drawn in this room, giving it a curious darkness against the bright sunlight outside. It was as if this young girl was afraid to face the brightness of the real world. The furnishings, Harry noted, were old but neat, and well kept.

"What do you want from me, Mr. Mercer?" the girl asked. Her voice was low-pitched, barely audible.

"The truth, Miss Sanfilippo."

"And what good will that do? The police already know the truth. It has been told to them."

"My paper—"

"Your paper prints what it wants to print," she interrupted.

She seemed so much older than she actually was, Harry thought, an impression strengthened by her innate calm dignity, qualities that he wished he could share at the moment. His stomach had tightened into a hard knot of excitement; he felt he was right on the brink of a whale of a good story, a story that would help people like this girl, and at the same time, one that would put a crimp in people like Lieutenant Skinner and Thomas Hennings. He was hoping for that.

"You live here alone with your brother?" he asked.

She moved slightly, her back ramrod straight. "My father lives with us. My mother is dead."

"Where's your father now?"

"Where he should be, at the police station. It will do him no good and he realizes this, yet he is there, all the same."

"Did you tell the police about those two, what they did to you?"

"Yes."

"And?"

"And what, Mr. Mercer?"

He leaned forward, resting his elbows on his knees. He would have given his last dollar right then for a good stiff drink.

"Look, Miss Sanfilippo," he said, "I'm only trying to do what I think is right."

Her eyes flickered slightly. A ghost of a smile hovered at her mouth corners, then was gone. "Perhaps you are, Mr. Mercer. I do not know. I know only that the situation is hopeless, that my brother and two others are at the police station, that a boy lies half-dead in the hospital because of what they did to him. That cannot be excused."

"But maybe it can be explained."

She sat very still for a long moment, then said: "The paper would not print the truth, Mr. Mercer."

"Maybe not. But if I can get you—and other witnesses—to back up what I write, then I can have the story printed in a national magazine."

For the first time since he had entered the room, the girl seemed to lose a little of her self-composure. She fiddled with her hands in her lap, looked away from Harry for a moment, then back again.

"I will give you what you want, Mr. Mercer."

"In writing?"

"If you wish."

"And the witnesses to what those boys did to you?"

"I will get that in writing, also."

"Did anyone hear you tell the police about what happened?"

"My father."

"Good. Very good." He rose, almost beside himself with elation. He would tie them in knots now; he had them right where it would hurt. "You're quite a young lady, Miss Sanfilippo."

"And you're quite a man, Mr. Mercer."

"I think maybe I will be, some day. My head has been a trifle over-sized the past few years."

She laughed at that, and it was a good sound.

At exactly ten minutes to six, Harry pulled up in front of the Hennings house and parked. He sat a moment, letting his nerves relax. He glanced down at the manila folder beside him, thought again of the long afternoon he had spent gathering and writing the material within that folder. He left the car and started up the walk.

Hennings answered the door. "You cut the deadline rather thin, Mercer," he said.

"It's not six o'clock yet," Harry answered.

"Have you finished the story?"

"Of course."

He followed Hennings into the living room. Mrs. Hennings sat in an easy chair, the picture of the sophisticated, upperclass housewife, proud of her husband, what he was doing, proud of his profession and status. Grace stood beside her sister.

She smiled at Harry and said, "I understand Thomas has been giving you a hard time."

"That's not true, Grace," Hennings said, "and you know it. I demand that those who work for me follow the instructions of the management. I don't believe that comes under the heading of giving them a hard time."

Harry handed the manila folder to Hennings. "Here's the story," he said.

Hennings sat down on a couch to read it. Harry watched him carefully for the reaction he was certain the story would get. He had left out nothing, telling how the boys had attacked Angelina Sanfilippo, how she had told the police of this, even of how he had argued with Hennings on how the story should be handled.

"This is ridiculous and absurd," Hennings said angrily

when he had finished. "You don't really expect me to print this, do you, Mercer?"

"That's up to you."

"But it—it's an indictment of myself."

Grace took the story from her brother-in-law, began reading it.

"This finishes you, Mercer. You're washed up. I don't want to see you at the office again. We'll mail your check."

"Have it your way."

"Harry," Grace said, "how could you? You ought to know that this kind of story won't do anyone any good."

He reached across, taking the folder from her. "I thought you would say that."

Hennings said, "You can't expect to rationalize away an attack that almost caused a boy to lose his life—"

"Then he's okay now?" Harry asked.

"—Yes, yes, he's okay," Hennings continued. "But he was almost killed, and that's the point of this whole thing. We can't let these people get away with homicidal acts like this."

"What people?" Harry asked calmly.

"Those people down there!" Hennings almost yelled. "They can't take the law into their own hands and—"

"That's what you're doing, isn't it?" Harry interrupted.

Hennings looked at him silently for a moment. "I think you'd better go now, Mercer. I've just about had my fill of you."

"Harry, please," Grace said. "What good will a story like this do?"

"Think of what it would do to the poor boys' families," Mrs. Hennings put in. "All that shame."

"And what about the families of those three down at the police station?" asked Harry.

"I don't think that's a very reasonable attitude, Mr. Mercer," Mrs. Hennings said.

"I told you to get out of my house," Hennings said. "Now please go at once."

"I'm going. But before I do, I think you should know that I've already received an okay on this story from the national picture magazine. And I'm afraid, when the photographers and reporters tell their story, Beach City will look pretty sick."

He saw the shocked looks on their faces as he turned and left the house. He was happy. A door had closed behind him—another door was opening. A door to freedom. He remembered his first interview with Hennings—perhaps now that he was his own boss, he would have to revise his drinking schedule. Getting drunk every two weeks might not be worth the trouble.

Grace came running out of the house, catching up with him as he reached his car. She put a hand on his arm, holding him.

"Harry—" she said.

"We have nothing to say to each other."

"Because of what just happened?"

"No."

"But the other will work itself out, Harry. I know it will."

"I know it will, too." He looked at her almost tenderly. He felt sorry for her, which was not the emotion she wanted from him. "You'll find a man one of these days, Grace, the right man for you."

"You're that man, Harry."

"Maybe you think so right this minute, but you're wrong and you'll realize it before long. You belong in there with them—" and he motioned his head to the house— "and I belong—well, certainly not in there."

"Drive me home, Harry. We'll talk there."

"I'm not going that way."

"You're being stubborn."

"I always have been stubborn."

"If you drove me home," she said, glancing over her shoulder, like a small girl making a secret pact against her parent's wishes, "I'll prove to you that I'm a woman.

All the way this time, Harry. No backing out. It'll be just as you want."

"I already have what I want," he said.

He got into the car and eyed the rear-view mirror as he drove off. She was still standing there, one hand raised as if she intended waving to him. He smiled. She would be all right. Her kind always was.

Bess grinned happily at him as he entered. "Your head doesn't look very bloody," she said.

"This time I didn't lose."

"Good for you."

"Still love me, Bess?"

"Always and always. How's the waistline?"

"I haven't eaten since breakfast."

"You want dinner now, or—"

"I think I'll take dinner later."

They were laughing as they ran into the bedroom.

THE END